combatant outside the arena is punishable by death.

5.   The right to make a ritual cut is earned by disabling

o...

6.   T... ...ual cut
     t... ...sed to
     i...

7. An unseemly cowardly reaction to the ritual cut after combat is punishable by a three-month ban from the arena. Bravery is mandatory.

8. Simulacra, commonly known as lacs, are used in both attack and defence of the human combatants.

9. The min combatant fights behind one lac; the mag combatant fights behind three lacs.

10. For the first five minutes combatants must fight behind their lacs. Then the warning gong sounds and they must change position and fight in front of them, where they are more vulnerable to the blades of their opponent.

11. A lac is disabled when a blade is inserted in its throat-socket. This calls the wurde *endoff*; the lac collapses and becomes inert.

12. Arena 13 combatants may also fight under **Special Rules**.

SPECIAL RULES

1. **Grudge match rules**
    The objective of a grudge match is to kill one's opponent. All **Primary Rules** apply, but for the following changes:
    - If blood is spilled during combat, hostilities need not cease; the fight continues.
    - After an opponent's lac or lacs have been disabled, the opponent is slain. The throat may be slit, or the head severed from the neck – the decision belongs to the victor. The death blow is carried out by either the victorious human combatant or his lac.
    - Alternatively the victor may grant clemency in return for an apology or an agreed financial penalty.

2. **Trainee Tournament rules**

The objective of this tournament is to advance the training of first-year trainees by pitting them against their peers in Arena 13. For the protection of the trainees and to mitigate the full rigour of Arena 13 contests, there are two changes to the **Primary Rules**:
- The whole contest must be fought behind the lacs.
- Kransin is not used on blades for the ritual cut.

3. **A challenge from Hob**
- When Hob visits Arena 13 to make a challenge, a min combatant must fight him on behalf of the Wheel.
- All min combatants must assemble in the Green Room, where that combatant will be chosen by lottery.
- Grudge match rules apply, but for one: there is no clemency.
- The fight is to the death. If the human combatant is beaten then, alive or dead, he may be taken away by Hob. Combatants, spectators and officials must not interfere.

SECONDARY RULES

1. Blades must not be carried into the Green Room or the changing room.
2. No Arena 13 combatant may fight with blades outside the arena. An oath must be taken at registration to abide by that rule. Any infringement shall result in a lifetime ban from Arena 13 combat.
3. Spitting in the arena is forbidden.
4. Cursing and swearing in the arena is forbidden.
5. Abuse of one's opponent during combat is forbidden.
6. In the case of any dispute, the Chief Marshal's decision is absolute. There can be no appeal.

Also available by Joseph Delaney

ARENA 13

THE WARRIOR

JOSEPH DELANEY

RED FOX

RED FOX

UK | USA | Canada | Ireland | Australia
India | New Zealand | South Africa

Red Fox is part of the Penguin Random House group of companies
whose addresses can be found at global.penguinrandomhouse.com.

www.penguin.co.uk
www.puffin.co.uk
www.ladybird.co.uk

Penguin
Random House
UK

First published 2017
001

Text copyright © Joseph Delaney, 2017
Arena 13 branding by James Fraser, 2017
Map illustration in Chapter 4 by Matt Jones, 2017

The moral right of the author has been asserted

Set in 11/14 Bell MT by Jouve (UK), Milton Keynes
Printed in Great Britain by Clays Ltd, St Ives plc

A CIP catalogue record for this book is available from the British Library

ISBN: 978–1–782–95407–1

All correspondence to:
Red Fox
Penguin Random House Children's
80 Strand, London WC2R 0RL

For Marie

The dead do dream.

They dream of the world of Nym and twist hopelessly
within its dark labyrinths,
seeking that which they can never reach.
But for a few, a very few, a wurde is called.
It is a wurde that summons them again to life.

Cursed are the twice-born.

Amabramsum: the Genthai Book of Wisdom

PROLOGUE

MATH

When Math glimpsed the west bank of the River Medie, his heart soared. He was almost home. Ahead, in the far distance, was the Barrier that enclosed Midgard, a black mass of cloud and mist that reached from the ground high into the sky, writing and churning as if it was alive.

It had been created by the djinn after they defeated and destroyed the Human Empire in a great battle long ago. Now the last few thousand humans were trapped within it, permitted to live out their little lives as long as they did not attempt to cross.

Soon he would be back within that Barrier, safe from those who pursued him – or so he thought.

But now Math glanced back and, to his dismay, saw riders watching him from the top of the rise, dark silhouettes against the grey sky. They had caught him at last.

He counted them quickly. There were thirteen.

In truth, twenty-six, not thirteen, creatures were watching

him. Advancing down the hill towards him were barska and orla – binary djinn, each a double entity. Each barsk rode an orl, a creature with a massive head covered in dark scales, its double row of teeth angled slightly backwards into a mouth dripping with silver saliva. It ran upon two sturdy legs, and its elongated hands had four fingers and an opposable thumb. Each digit terminated in a murderous sharp talon.

Their riders, the barska, were even more daunting. Although roughly human in shape, each had four arms. Two were used to grip black spurs of bone jutting from the armoured neck of the orl, while two gripped weapons: a spear and a blade.

The barska wore black armour and leather gloves. The head was covered with a conical helmet, a nasal strip protecting the nose. Only the face was vulnerable to the three weapons carried by Math – a short sword, a shield and a bow. The round shield was not merely for defence; its rim was razor-sharp and could inflict terrible damage on an adversary.

Math was on foot and would be hard-pressed to defeat just one such binary djinni. Against thirteen such entities he stood no chance at all. He was as good as dead.

For weeks he had been journeying back towards his home-land of Midgard. Under cover of darkness, he had made his way south, knowing that he would be followed by the barska and orla, the deadly servants of the powerful asscka djinn who dwelt north of the High Wall; knowing that he would be slain.

For he had done something that was forbidden to all humans – he had dared to cross the Barrier. The penalty for that was death.

In addition to fleeing for his life, he had performed one

important task. He had drawn a map detailing the route he had taken. He would give it to his people, the Genthai. One day they hoped to ride across the Barrier, defeat the djinn and, by force of arms, take back for humans the whole world. His map would show them the way.

So now, at last, they had caught him. He was so close to home – but not close enough. He would die on the riverbank, within sight of the Barrier that enclosed his homeland.

But then Math was given a sliver of hope. The line of djinn halted and only a single barsk and orl charged down the slope towards him.

Did they have some sense of honour? Would they only fight him one at a time? he wondered.

Math placed his sword and shield at his feet, nocked an arrow to his bow, drew it back and tensed, holding his breath. He waited calmly for a target to present itself.

The djinn was almost upon him when that target became visible.

His arrow flew fast and true, and found the eye to the left of the helmet's nose guard, burying itself right up to the flight feathers. It had gone deep into the brain, and the barsk fell backwards off its mount, all four arms convulsing and desperately reaching for the arrow.

Math dropped his bow, and just had time to take up his sword and shield before the orl reached him. He rolled aside, and its two massive feet thundered past before circling to come at him again. He noted that the barsk was still on the ground, writhing in what seemed to be its death throes.

But the orl was a formidable opponent, the massive dinosaur head swinging from side to side as it bore down on him, the thin arms and taloned hands reaching out, ready to rend and tear his flesh. He used the curved edge of his shield to slice away those arms just short of the elbow. They spurted black blood, and the orl let out a scream.

He spun away from it, but not before lunging for its face with his sword. The weapon went deep into the bridge of its nose, slicing across both eyes. The orl ran on unsteadily, the stumps of its arms still spraying blood. It blundered blindly on into the river and, within seconds, still shrieking, had been borne away by the fast current.

The sounds of distress grew fainter and fainter, until all was silent. Math stared up at his enemies. No doubt they hadn't expected him to be victorious. But before he'd ever fought in Arena 13, Math had been a warrior, skilled in the use of sword and bow.

It was too much to hope for – to face another single barsk – and indeed the creatures moved down the slope in two columns to encircle him. Slowly that circle tightened as they advanced. Math spun on his heels, still holding up his shield and his sword, but it seemed likely that they would all attack at once. The best he could do was inflict some damage on one of his enemies.

As he moved, Math was aware of the weakness in his left leg – the old injury he'd received in Arena 13. It reduced his mobility, and the long walk had put it under increasing strain.

It was then that the light suddenly faded. The sun was hidden by cloud, but it was close to noon and the sky had been bright. Why was it suddenly becoming so dark? he wondered.

Math didn't dare take his eyes off his enemies, but he noticed that the barska and orla were no longer looking at him. They were staring up at the dark cloud, which was descending rapidly.

Math glanced upwards too, and felt a moment of fear. He knew what it was. That dense black cloud was swooping down like a flock of birds, though it was something far more deadly.

These winged creatures were the gungara, creatures of the djinn that were used to devour and absorb the mind and tissue of their enemies. The barska and orla had no doubt summoned them. Within seconds, he reflected, only his skeleton would remain.

Instinctively, but knowing that it was useless, Math held his shield above his head. All around him he heard the beating of wings. He thought they had come for him, but to his surprise they attacked the enemies that surrounded him. He glimpsed jaws and teeth dripping with blood, and heard the shrieks of the barska and orla as they were shredded and devoured. He knew that djinn often fought djinn – these gungara must be the enemies of those who had attacked him.

Math still feared that they would come for him next, and waited for those teeth to sink into his own flesh. He was afraid but resigned. He took a deep breath and waited for death.

But nothing happened.

He crouched there, still holding the shield above his head, as the darkness gradually gave way to light again. The gungara were taking flight, soaring upwards, leaving him untouched.

Math looked at the ground around him. It was soaked in black blood; despite their scaly armour, the flesh of the barska and orla had been stripped, leaving only bloody bones. And the eye-sockets of each entity had been split open, the eyes torn out and the brains devoured.

But why had he been spared?

He stared up at the dark flock of gungara wheeling above. Suddenly they formed a distinct shape against the light grey of the clouds. That shape was unmistakable. It was the head of a wolf.

The gungara belonged to a lupina djinni – the Trader Math had been travelling with before being forced to flee.

The Trader had saved him.

Now he could go home and give the map to his people.

Math was the great hero of Arena 13. He had defeated Hob fifteen times before being forced to retire because of his injury.

But that was in the past. Now he had a future: he was destined to marry a woman called Shola, whom he would love more than life itself. They would have a son called Leif. Math would enjoy twelve years of happiness before the evil djinn Hob slew his wife and brought about his own death.

But his son would survive and live on to fight in Arena 13.

Leif would seek revenge for what had been done to his family.

THE DEATH GAMBIT

The Mihalick Manoeuvre is the riskiest tactic for
any human combatant. It invariably results in death
or maiming.

The Manual of Trigladius Combat

LEIF

It was the last night of the Arena 13 season.

Somewhere out of sight a bass drum began to beat like a throbbing heart. As the huge thirteen-branched candelabrum descended, illuminating Arena 13 with yellow light, Pyncheon, the Chief Marshal, appeared to announce the first of the evening's contests. He wore a broad red sash over his black gown, and carried a long thin silver trumpet.

He remained the highest authority here in the Wheel, but things had changed. Although he still strutted across the arena and was a member of the expanded Wheel Directorate that now ruled Gindeen, he'd lost much of his power.

Pyncheon had always been arrogant. I smiled to myself as I thought of the distaste with which he would view this first contest on tonight's List.

The tiers of plush red-leather seats were packed to capacity, with almost as many women as men among the spectators.

An anticipatory hush had fallen over the gallery. We could now hear the sound of boots approaching the minos door of the arena, through which the combatants fighting with one lac entered. My heart thudded in my chest as the first combatant entered ahead of the armoured lac. It was Kwin.

She walked forward confidently and stood facing the Chief Marshal before taking up her combat position behind her lac. Lacs wore full metal armour and were strong and fast, their manoeuvres guided by the patterns placed within their minds. The only way they could be downed was when a blade was inserted into their throat-socket, which was held in place by an iron collar. This called up a patterning wurde called *endoff*, which immediately brought the lac crashing to the arena floor.

The spectators were here to see history made, and my mouth was dry with excitement and fear.

I was not afraid for myself. I had fought and won my final contest the previous evening. I was just a spectator. I was afraid for Kwin – although I was excited for her too.

I knew how much this meant to her: she was about to fight in Arena 13, the first female ever to do so.

The audience erupted with excitement. There was wild cheering, and they began to stamp their boots on the floor. Kwin smiled up towards the gallery. She knew where I'd be sitting and her eyes sought mine. She waved at me and I waved back enthusiastically, pleased that her dream of fighting in Arena 13 was finally being realized.

Then, as the first roar from the spectators began to

subside, there was a new sound that caused the smile to slip from Kwin's face.

A group of middle-aged men seated in the front row began to boo. There were some in Gindeen who wished to keep to the old ways. The last thing they wanted was for women to be the equal of men. Some claimed their jobs were at risk; others that it was improper and against female nature to fight in Arena 13.

But the women of Gindeen were out in force tonight and they began to cheer Kwin enthusiastically, chanting her name and blocking out the boos. They were dressed in silken finery, and most had painted their lips the traditional black – though a significant number had adopted the style first used by Kwin. She painted only her top lip black; the lower lip was the rich red colour of arterial blood.

Her opponent, a man named Rubico, now entered the arena through the other, larger, door, the magus, with his three lacs. Both Kwin and Rubico wore the regulation leather shorts and jerkin, their flesh open to the blade, and you won a contest by cutting your opponent.

Kwin looked beautiful, and I knew that her soul must be singing with joy.

Although women had previously been forbidden to fight in Arena 13, the brave and spirited Kwin had fought one of the lacs, blade against blade, in her father's cellar. She had won, but she had also been cut. Now, her hair was cut short on one side to reveal the scar because she looked upon it as a badge of honour. She was also proud of the *13* she'd had tattooed on her forehead. That fight had demonstrated her courage. Now the recent political turmoil and shifts of power had turned custom on its head. History was about to be made.

My friend Deinon, who was also a trainee, was seated on my left. He was staring down into the arena, his face full of concern. Kwin was his friend too and he really cared about her. But she was much more than that to me.

Pyncheon held up his hands and gazed at the gallery. 'Let it begin!' he called out, moving towards the mag door. There he paused and lifted the trumpet to his lips. There was a high, shrill note, and then the two doors rumbled shut.

This was the signal to begin, and the combatants rushed towards each other.

For a moment my heart was in my mouth. As they came together, I suddenly became aware of a faint odour, almost hidden by the perfume worn by the women in the audience. It was the stench of blood.

The floorboards below us were stained with it – both old and new. Only this season, four combatants had been slain. Three had been accidental deaths; one the result of a grudge match – which were fought to the death. My blood had also stained that floor. I had fought the djinn, Hob, and defeated him. But he had cut off my right ear.

You got accustomed to that smell, but it reminded you that combatants sometimes died in Arena 13. Now Kwin was down there, and blades were seeking her flesh.

There was a clash of metal against armour, the glint of blades as lac fought lac, human combatants dancing behind them. Attack and retreat, attack and retreat – this was the pattern as Kwin launched her single lac against her opponent, with his three.

My fear faded and I smiled with satisfaction. She was slowly driving Rubico's tri-glad backwards. This was no mean feat; although no older than thirty, he was a veteran of the arena and was ranked in the top third of magus combatants, those who fought with three lacs.

For five minutes they would fight behind their lacs. Then a gong would sound and, after a short pause, they would move in front. This was much more dangerous, and Kwin would then be vulnerable both to the blades of her opponent and to those of his three lacs.

I hoped she'd win before that stage was reached.

I licked my lips nervously and looked at Tyron, who was sitting on my right. He was staring down into the arena, watching his daughter fight. He couldn't keep still – fidgeting in his seat and rapping his fingers against his knees. He was the best artificer in Gindeen, and I was a trainee in his stable of fighters. Tyron had also replaced Pyncheon as Head of the Wheel Directorate. He was now one of the most important men in the city.

Just to his right sat Ada, who had patterned Kwin's lac. She had once been the High Adept of the Imperial Academy and was twice-born: she had died hundreds of years ago and was reborn into the false flesh from which all djinn are formed, still retaining her brilliance as a patterner. She had been the first woman to pattern a lac to fight in Arena 13 – and her skills were such that she made it sentient. She'd named that lac Thrym, and we'd fought together to defeat one of Hob's selves in the arena.

The lac that now defended Kwin was not sentient. Still, I hoped that Ada had made it good enough to ensure Kwin's victory.

I began to feel nervous again, my concern for Kwin

growing. The aim was not to kill one's opponent, merely to draw blood, but accidents did happen. I gritted my teeth and thrust that thought from my mind.

There was a roar of approval from the gallery. Kwin and her lac had driven her opponents right back against the arena wall and they were struggling to escape. The women began to cheer and stamp their feet, and there were shrieks of delight. Kwin was very fast: she was using Ulum – signalling to her lac by drumming her boots on the arena floor – and positioning it perfectly so that it could use its blades effectively.

'Good girl! Good girl!' I heard Tyron exclaim as we heard that metallic sound, signifying that a blade had struck the iron collar of an opposing lac, almost entering the throat-slit. Any moment now Kwin must surely prevail. The five minutes were almost up. Soon the gong would sound for a pause in the fighting. Then the human combatants would re-position themselves, fighting head to head, with their lacs behind them. They would both be more vulnerable. Both could be cut badly.

Tyron was leaning forward, drumming his fingers on the rail now, his face anxious. 'Now, Kwin! Finish it now, girl!' he said.

At first he had been against his daughter fighting in the arena. It had taken Ada weeks to persuade him to allow it. No doubt he was now regretting that decision.

Suddenly there were jeers from the front row of the gallery. They came from that group of boorish men. Then there was a flash of red, and Kwin's lac appeared to be covered in blood.

My heart leaped with fear. Had Rubico been cut? Or was it Kwin?

The audience was stunned into silence, but then there was a burst of raucous laughter. I glanced across and saw that one of the men was holding a metal container that dripped a red liquid.

It was paint, not blood, I realized. He had thrown it in protest against a female fighting in the arena. It had caused serious damage to Kwin's lac, penetrating the horizontal slit in its helmet and blinding it.

It staggered backwards, almost colliding with her. The creature couldn't see well enough to defend itself.

The contest should be halted, I thought. How could it be allowed to continue? I listened for the trumpet, but Pyncheon was unmoved – though he was watching and surely knew what had happened.

In a second a blade would call endoff on Kwin's lac; she would lose and be forced to accept the ritual cut to signify her defeat.

What happened next brought Tyron to his feet.

It was so quick that I almost missed it. Kwin stepped in front of her lac and dived forward, still holding her blades. She did a forward roll between the legs of the opposing tri-glad.

My heart was in my mouth as blades stabbed down at her. I didn't want to watch but I couldn't tear my eyes away. What Kwin had done was incredibly brave, but she had taken a terrible risk.

Somehow she avoided those blades. Then she was past the opposing lacs, still rolling. With the blade in her left hand, she struck at Rubico's legs and cut him below the knee.

A second later a blade found the throat-slit of her own lac to call endoff. But Kwin had already drawn blood. She had won her first contest — though at great risk to her life.

The applause was thunderous. I was on my feet, clapping and cheering at the top of my voice. Deinon and I slapped each other on the back in amazement and relief — but Tyron shook his head, wiping the sweat from his brow with the back of his hand. He had probably aged ten years in the last few minutes.

Assistant marshals were already striding down the far aisle to arrest the group of men who had thrown the paint. I hoped they would be fined and banned from the gallery for a very long time.

We went back to Tyron's house for a small celebratory end-of-season party. Deinon and I were still living there while our training continued. We shared the accommodation with Tyron and his two daughters, Kwin and Teena, and Teena's son, Robbie.

'You are to be congratulated, daughter, on winning your first contest in Arena 13,' Tyron said, raising his glass in a toast. 'But don't you ever dare do *that* again! I have enough grey hairs already!'

There was a chink of glasses and cries of approval and congratulation. But, despite his apparent joviality, I could see the tension in Tyron's face. His hair was already grey, shaved to little more than stubble; the lines around his eyes were deepening and advancing towards his cheeks.

I knew how he'd felt. My heart had lurched when Kwin

rolled through the legs of the lacs. I thought I was going to lose her.

She had performed what was known as the Mihalick Manoeuvre, commonly known as the Death Gambit. It was named after the man who'd first used the tactic. Mihalick was the only one who survived and won. Five other combatants had attempted the manoeuvre since. Four had died, cut to ribbons by the blades of their opponent's lacs; the fifth had been badly maimed. He now hobbled along with a stick and had lost the use of his left arm.

I knew that Kwin had been desperate to win her first contest, but she shouldn't have taken such a risk. I was annoyed with her for putting her life on the line, but even more annoyed with Pyncheon, the Chief Marshal. He should have stopped the fight the moment the paint landed on the lac's head. No doubt he wanted to see Kwin lose.

Tyron would be having a word with him. He'd also given his daughter a private telling-off. But Kwin was Kwin: she always did what she wanted. There was no way she would allow herself to be defeated in her first contest in Arena 13.

I looked around the room. There were about thirty people at the party: artificers like Tyron, including the bushy-browed Brid and the lanky, awkward Wode, who were close colleagues, each with his own stable of combatants. They had put their lives at risk in our failed attempt to destroy every one of Hob's selves after I'd defeated him with Thrym.

That was a threat that Kwin, fortunately, hadn't had to face tonight. Hob, the djinni who lived in a thirteen-spired citadel on the hill above the city, could visit at any time to challenge those who fought in Arena 13. Normally a lottery decided which human combatant would fight him. So Kwin might have been chosen.

But things had changed. Generally I did not summon Thrym to fight in the arena, but it had been agreed that, should Hob visit, I would be the one to face him. Thrym would wait below, ready for such an eventuality.

Together, we had beaten Hob once, and we could do it again.

Following the removal of the Protector, who had been put in place by the djinn who dwelt beyond the Barrier to rule over Midgard, people had waited fearfully. Some believed that hordes of monstrous djinn would charge through the Barrier to slaughter us all. A city militia had been formed to complement the Genthai army, but nothing had happened.

People were also afraid of Hob. He had preyed upon the city for centuries – though since the fall of the Protector he'd killed nobody; nor had he visited the Wheel to issue a challenge. We'd thought that the djinn had appointed the Protector as sole ruler. But after his fall it had been revealed that a *dual* authority had governed Midgard; Hob had been the other ruler.

So why hadn't he intervened in some way? I wondered. His silence and inaction were unnerving. People believed that he possessed terrible weapons of destruction; many feared that he might use them against Gindeen.

At first the fearful inhabitants had stayed indoors as much as possible, but the city needed food, and soon farmers started to deliver their produce and bring their cattle to the slaughterhouse again. Life had returned to an uneasy routine.

My eyes searched the room. A few combatants had come to the party; some of them I'd fought in the arena since defeating Hob. I'd ended the season in the top third – which wasn't bad considering I'd had so few contests. Next year I hoped that Tyron would allow me to fight twice a week right through the season. Then I'd have a real chance of coming first in the rankings.

My father, Math, had been Arena 13's best fighter. My aim was to match his achievement and, if I got the chance, to defeat Hob over and over again.

I was watching Tyron's guests when Deinon came across to join me.

'I'm off very early tomorrow, Leif,' he said with a smile. 'I won't even have time for breakfast. I have to go and help on the farm.'

'So soon?' I asked.

'I've little choice, I'm afraid. My family need an extra pair of hands.'

The farm had been going through a bad patch. This season Deinon's father had been unable to pay for his son's training, but Tyron had generously waived the fee. He really believed in Deinon, who showed great promise as a patterner, using wurdes of Nym to shape and improve the lacs. I had speed, quick reflexes and strength – skills that were good for the arena; Deinon had brains, and would one day make a great artificer, with his own stable of combatants.

'What will you do, Leif?' Deinon asked.

Last year I'd gone to visit the Genthai, but I had no plans to do so again. I was half Genthai, half city dweller, but increasingly I had felt the tug of my father's people. They were warriors who dwelt in the forest and had no fear of Hob. One day they hoped to cross the Barrier, defeat the djinn and reclaim the whole world for humans. It seemed a hopeless task, but they truly believed that it could be done.

Since then some of the Genthai had left their forest. Their leader, Konnit, and many of his warriors were now based in the east wing of the Protector's palace, where the Ruling Council met. Others patrolled close to the city. As time passed, it seemed less likely that the djinn would attack, but defensive strategies were being drawn up.

'Tyron's asked me to stay here and carry on with light training right through the autumn and winter. It sounds good to me. And it means that I'll be close to Kwin,' I said with a smile.

'Lucky you!' Deinon laughed.

I *was* lucky – very lucky – to have Kwin. I was looking forward to spending time with her during the long winter. I was looking forward to the training too. I wanted to perfect my performance so as to be ready if Hob came to fight again. The djinni possessed one mind but many selves. Defeating and killing one of them in Arena 13 would not only diminish the threat he presented, it would give me great satisfaction. It was Hob who had brought about the deaths of my parents. I wanted to hurt him as much as I could.

We both glanced across at Kwin. She was talking to Ada, who was now an artificer in her own right, although she shared Tyron's training facilities and lived here. So far she only had a stable of one – Kwin – but she was also helping with Deinon's training as a patterner.

As I watched, Teena, Tyron's elder daughter, joined them.

They chatted briefly and then went off to talk to the other guests. I felt a twinge of disappointment. I wouldn't get a chance to be alone with Kwin until the next day.

However, I consoled myself with the thought that we would be together for the whole autumn and winter.

But it was not to be.

A DANGEROUS INVITATION

I began to feel as if I was the expression of a higher
power, an aspect of Nym, the goddess of all pattern,
movement and dance.

The Testimony of Math

LEIF

Early the following morning, soon after I'd waved Deinon
off, a visitor called at the house.

It was a warrior with a summons from the leader of the
Genthai. Konnit wanted to see me right away. Breakfast
would have to wait.

I walked across the city to the east wing of the palace. I
found Konnit alone, sitting at a long table. I sat down opposite him.

While Tyron had aged during the last year, Konnit looked
younger. His moustache was a rich brown – the same colour
as his long hair – his face was decorated with the full Genthai tattoos, and he radiated strength and purpose.

He welcomed me with a smile. 'First, Leif, I must congratu-
late you on the part you played in bringing the negotiations

between the Genthai and the City Directorate to a successful conclusion so that we now have a joint Ruling Council.'

'Thank you, lord,' I said, bowing to him.

'I would like to invite you to join a small expedition we are planning. Note that I "invite"; I do not command you. It will be very dangerous and you and the other Genthai warriors will be away for at least three months – maybe longer. The purpose is to carry out some reconnaissance beyond the Barrier.'

I looked at Konnit in amazement. Everyone considered the Barrier to be an insuperable obstacle. Even to approach it drove some men insane. That high, swirling wall of mist and fear kept us confined. Only the Trader crossed it with impunity – and he did so by ship. Moreover he was not a prisoner of the Barrier; his home lay somewhere beyond it.

'You look astonished, Leif!' said Konnit.

'I am!' I replied. 'I thought it was impossible for anyone to leave Midgard.'

'There is a way, but it is dangerous, and not everyone survives. Even when you're across, you run the risk of encountering djinn; no one has ever ventured that far. But this time it will be different. This expedition will probe further.'

'Will we go by sea, lord?' I asked.

Konnit shook his head and smiled. 'The journey will be overland.'

'What's it like, lord – beyond the Barrier?' I wondered.

'In terms of landforms, flora and fauna, everything is very much the same as here. But who knows what may await us further afield? Up until now our warriors have not encountered any djinn. This time things may be different – though we hope to learn more about the djinn without being detected – and to find the route that best suits our army when the time comes to attack them.'

'Will there not be djinn guarding against humans who try to escape Midgard?' I asked.

'Indeed there might be, Leif. There are none close to the Barrier, but further out – who knows? However, any knowledge we gain about the djinn will help us to defeat them. Even Ada knows nothing of them as they are *now*; she fears that they may have advanced both in number and in the technology at their disposal: we must find out if this is so. And think of this, Leif: any such knowledge might well help us to defeat Hob.'

My mind was in a whirl. I'd been looking forward to spending the winter with Kwin, and to developing my combat skills. Yet this was too good an opportunity to miss. I'd always wondered what lay beyond the Barrier – as did anyone who was confined within it. Now I had the chance to find out. It was an adventure that called out to me – and might also bring me closer to destroying Hob and avenging the deaths of my parents.

Somewhere deep within me the decision was made, and I spoke without thinking.

'I'd like to go,' I told Konnit.

'Then be ready at dawn tomorrow. You will travel north, and receive weapons training on the way.'

That was a shock! I'd agreed to go, but little did I imagine that it would be straight away. I was dismayed. I'd hoped for more time with Kwin while preparations were made for the crossing.

However, I had said yes now and must stand by my decision. After all, a desire for revenge had brought me to Gindeen in the first place. Hob must be destroyed, and that had to take precedence over everything else.

'How will we get through the Barrier, lord?' I wanted to know.

'The crossing carries the risk of madness or death. However, we have guides – Genthai mystics, known as Medes, who inhabit the lands close to the Barrier and are sensitive to its fluctuations. They take their name from the River Medie. The best entry and exit point lies on its bank. .

'The strength of the Barrier varies depending on the cycles of the moon. By taking advantage of its phases, the Medes cross in relative safety – though they do not always guide other people through successfully. There will be ten of you on this expedition. We do not expect all ten to pass through the Barrier safely.'

'Why me, lord?' I asked.

'Why shouldn't it be you, Leif? This is an important assignment, and you've shown yourself worthy to be a part of it. You defeated a werewight and bested Hob in combat. Besides, your presence was requested by the leader of the expedition – Garrett.'

I knew Garrett. The big warrior had supervised my work when I'd visited the Genthai lands the previous winter. He'd had me felling trees until my hands were blistered. At first he'd bullied me both verbally and physically. But later he'd told me that this harsh treatment had been a test, part of the initiation of a Genthai returning to the tribe after exile.

When we'd broken out of a prison in the Protector's palace, I'd also fought alongside him and opened a gate to let the

Genthai army in. I was pleased that Garrett had chosen me. It was an honour.

My first task was to break the news to Kwin and her father.

I went to see Tyron first – though I had to wait as he was in his office in the admin building.

Now, well after dark, we were in his study at the top of his house. On the desk before him stood a glass of red wine.

'It'll be dangerous, boy,' he said, scratching the stubble on top of his head. 'You're risking your life. If the djinn get the faintest whiff of the expedition, you're all as good as dead. We might never see you again.'

'It's a risk I'm prepared to take,' I told him. 'All my life I've wanted to see what's beyond the Barrier. My father sailed there with the Trader. I've no knowledge of what he saw or experienced. Now I'd like to see it too.'

'I thought you wanted to destroy Hob. I thought you sought revenge for the deaths of your parents. Isn't that more important?' Tyron asked, leaning towards me.

'I still want that – I'm ready to face Hob in Arena 13 again. But there'll be no more combat until next season. I'll be back for that. Konnit believes that we'll gain valuable information about the djinn – things that even Ada doesn't know. That knowledge might also be used to understand how to deal with Hob.'

'Well, it's a very risky journey, and I fear for your safety – though, having said that, at least you'll be out of Hob's reach. He's been quiet recently, but he might well take revenge for our attempt on his life. You're the one who defeated him in the arena, Leif. You're high on his list of targets. At least beyond the Barrier you'll be safe from him.'

I left Tyron frowning and sipping his wine and went to talk to Kwin.

I knocked on her bedroom door and she bade me enter.

She was sitting in a low chair in front of a mirror, combing her hair. She always wore it the same way – long on one side but short on the other, to reveal the scar she'd earned fighting one of her father's lacs.

I knelt beside her and stared at my own reflection. The left side of my face bore the moko, the Genthai tattoo – deeply etched lines and whorls following its contours. That showed my heritage through the bloodline of my father, Math. The right side was unadorned because my mother, Shola, had not been Genthai. I was a half-blood, sitting between the two races, but this very fact had meant that I could act as Mediator and steer the negotiations between the city dwellers and the Genthai to a successful conclusion.

On the right, my hair was shaved to a dark stubble – to draw attention to my missing ear; Hob had cut it off during our fight. That had been Kwin's idea. Like her scar, she considered it to be a badge of courage – something to show off. I looked at her beautiful face in the mirror, with the number 13 tattooed on her forehead. Our eyes met and she smiled at me.

I tried to smile back, but I saw her eyes fill with alarm. It was hard to hide anything from Kwin.

'What's wrong?' she asked.

So I told her.

'Tomorrow? So soon? No! No, Leif, no!' she cried. 'I might never see you again.'

I was taken aback by her reaction. Kwin had always been so strong and independent; she wasn't given to displays of emotion like this. But then she turned away from me and was silent for a while, considering the matter. Eventually she looked at me again, and I saw that her face was filled with strength and purpose.

'You know what?' she said. 'I'm jealous. I wish I was going. I'd love to explore the lands beyond the Barrier!'

We hugged each other tightly and I tried to reassure her.

'I wish you could come with us, but even if the Genthai agreed, your father would forbid it. But don't you worry – I'll be back for the start of next season. You won't get rid of me that easily!'

As I began to pack my things for the journey, I picked up my father's book and read the spine: *The Testimony of Math*.

I decided not to take it with me in case it got lost or damaged. It belonged to Tyron, and I intended to return it to him before I set off. The book contained detailed accounts of Math's training with Gunter, the greatest artificer of his time, and of each contest he had fought in Arena 13.

However, most of the narrative concerned the fifteen bouts he'd won against Hob. It was good to read about his achievements, but I was disappointed not to have an account of the journeys he was supposed to have made across the Barrier with the Trader; the period covered by the book was before this.

There was one short passage that I kept returning to again and again.

While in combat I began to experience strange states of conscious-
ness: it was as if I was floating, my arms and legs responding
instinctively; but these were not my usual fast reactions — I began
to feel as if I was the expression of a higher power, an aspect of
Nym, the goddess of all pattern, movement and dance.

I was no longer merely dancing the patterns of the Trigladius;
in some way I became those patterns.

I didn't believe in the goddess, but that did not matter. The
sensation was still there.

And, once again, that contest ended in the same way.
Hob lay there in two separate pieces in a pool of bright red blood.

It seemed that my father had experienced some kind of
altered consciousness — an almost mystical state. It was at
odds with the rest of his account, which was factual and
down to earth. There were those who really did believe that
Nym was a goddess, and muttered prayers to her before they
fought contests. But how could a patterning language be a
goddess? I wondered. It didn't make sense.

Next I took my leave of Ada. I told her about my father's
strange experience. After all, she knew more about Nym
than anyone else in Gindeen.

'Could Nym really be a goddess?' I asked.

To my surprise, Ada did not dismiss my question as foolish.
Far from it.

'Nym was worshipped and considered to be a goddess by
one religious sect,' she explained. 'In my day there was toler-
ance of all religious beliefs, however outlandish, and nobody
mocked them. Indeed, there were scientists who didn't dismiss the idea. They said it stood up to scrutiny.'

'Scientists believed that Nym was a goddess!' I exclaimed in astonishment.

Ada smiled. 'Not necessarily a goddess able to hurl thunderbolts and rule humans, but an entity with a high degree of sentience that might, under certain circumstances, communicate with us. They believed that any highly complex system composed of many interacting parts might develop awareness. *The Dictionary of Nym*, that essence of the language, is now used by patterners and coded into lacs. In my time it was also embedded into devices and structures that were as enduring as rock or concrete. Some of those repositories of Nym may still survive to this day.

'There is something else,' she continued. 'Those who worshipped Nym believed that she favoured certain people – the best and the brightest, the fastest and the deadliest. Your father was the greatest of all Arena 13 combatants; he defeated Hob and danced the patterns of the Trigladius with supreme skill. If the goddess exists, he would surely have been one of her favourites.'

I nodded and smiled. Perhaps there had been more substance to my father's experience than I'd allowed.

'Have you any advice to offer regarding the djinn we may encounter beyond the Barrier?' I asked.

'I wish I was coming with you, Leif, but both Tyron and Konnit forbid it. They think my knowledge and skill at coding is too important to risk in such a dangerous assignment. I would love to encounter the djinn and find out what they are like now. But you must avoid them. They strike quickly and few survive. Your only hope in such an encounter is to open a dialogue. They are rational beings, and it should be possible to communicate with them. That is the only advice I can give.'

That night I spent a few last precious hours with Kwin.

We returned to the place we had visited together on my first night as a new trainee. Kwin had given me a night-time tour of the city, which had ended with an ascent of the high dome above the Wheel.

Using her father's key, she led me up the long spiral stair-case inside the Wheel, where there was a smell of dust and ancient wood. It was a relief to emerge into the cool autumnal air. I looked up at the large gibbous moon, which bathed the city in pale light.

We completed our climb up the outside of the dome, holding on to the slender hand rail until we reached the apex where, like a sharp spear-tip, the broken flagpole jutted towards the sky.

Here we stopped, both slightly breathless, and looked about us in silence.

I was the first to speak.

'Did a flag ever fly here?' I asked Kwin, staring at the broken pole.

She shook her head. 'Maybe once, long ago, but nobody remembers it. It was probably broken off in a storm – though no one has thought of replacing it. Few but the vultures come up here now!' she said with a smile, glancing up to where they circled overhead. 'This is one of my favourite spots. What an amazing view!'

I gazed out over the city, my eyes drawn to the west, where I could see the silver shimmer of the sea and, beyond it, the great

Barrier that encircled Midgard and sealed it off from the outer world. That roiling wall of mist or cloud had been created by the djinn after the last battle had destroyed the Human Empire.

The humans of Midgard were counted in the thousands rather than the billions who once inhabited the whole Earth. But our numbers were growing and, unless we cut down the forests, which the Genthai would never permit, within a couple of generations our farms would be unable to produce sufficient food to feed us. It was galling to think that, beyond the Barrier, unknown acres of good agricultural land went untilled.

I was going to miss Kwin, but my heart surged with excitement at the thought that I would soon explore those lands.

Ada had told me that the djinn controlled their own evolution. So what were they like now? Similar to Hob or very different? How did they live? I wondered.

I looked northwards – at the only building in the city that wasn't made of wood. Before the defeat of the Protector, this stone palace with its marble pillars had been his. It was supposed to have been built before the fall of the Human Empire, pre-dating even the first of Gindeen's other buildings.

Finally I stared at the stone and bronze citadel on the summit of the hill above the city, with its thirteen twisted spires; this was Hob's lair.

Yes, I would journey beyond the Barrier, but somehow, after my return, I would find a way of dealing with that monster.

One way or another I intended to have my revenge upon the djinni who had killed my parents.

CROSSING THE BARRIER

It is inevitable that humans will one day travel
beyond the Barrier that confines them.

Some view that as an act of heroism; others see it
as a death-wish.

Amabramdata: the Genthai Book of Prophecy

LEIF

I spent almost a month training before we attempted to cross
the Barrier. Most of it took place in the afternoons and even-
ings as we journeyed towards the northern stretch of the
Barrier. We were in no hurry: our crossing had to coincide
with a particular phase of the moon.

After a couple of days I was already homesick and wondering why we had set off so early. I could have spent another
two weeks with Kwin.

However, Garrett explained that we had to be ready for
whatever faced us beyond the Barrier. In martial skills, I was
easily the weakest of our group, he pointed out. I had the
necessary speed and skill to fight in the arena, but as far as

riding, archery and swordplay went, I was a novice. The month would prepare me for what lay ahead.

There were ten of us. We practised fighting in pairs, and my partner was always Garrett. We began with the longsword. He was an expert, and much bigger and stronger than me. I was struggling.

After a couple of sessions he shook his head and took me aside. 'We're not making the best of your abilities, Leif. Maybe one day, when you reach your full height and strength, you'll manage this weapon,' he told me, 'but meanwhile I think you'll be better off with these . . .'

He gave me a short sword and a round shield; the latter was more than just a means of defence and could be used to deadly effect. It was three feet in diameter and its metal edge was as sharp as a razor. This combination of weapons was much more to my liking, for the sword was similar to the blades I wielded in Arena 13. Now my natural skills could be used to my advantage.

Of course, the shields we used for practice had wooden guards, but I was soon covered in bruises. However, by the end of the second week I could give as good as I got. The skills I'd developed in Arena 13 began to pay off. I used my speed to find the most advantageous position, using the Trigladius steps that a warrior such as Garrett had no knowledge of. He was finding it increasingly difficult to fend off my attacks, and I could dance out of his range with ease.

I also had a natural aptitude for two other Genthai martial skills: riding and archery.

I was introduced to my mount, a black mare called Laras, with dappling on her hind quarters and a patch of white below her right eye; she was fast and responsive and eager to please, and soon we could weave our way through dense woods at a full gallop.

My skill with the short bow also developed rapidly; by the end of the month my aim was as accurate from horseback as it was when I was on foot. My confidence increased by leaps and bounds. I began to feel more and more like a Genthai warrior.

'They say that your father had great skill with the bow, Leif,' Garrett told me. 'It seems that you've inherited that gift. You have a natural aptitude for combat. I'm pleased with the progress you've made. Despite our limited training time, you've come on well.'

I was delighted to hear his words of praise, but my weapons training soon came to an end.

Day by day we had been getting closer to the Barrier. I had noted that there were no longer any birds, animals or insects to be seen or heard in the forest. Until recently it had been teeming with life. Now the trees were stunted and bare.

Above, the Barrier reared up before us like a great beast; a curtain of darkness with flecks of white, boiling like water in a cauldron. It moaned and groaned, and at night it glowed with unearthly streaks of fire.

Nerves gnawed at my stomach. It was time to make that dangerous crossing.

The Mede guide had come to meet us, and told us what we had to do. We would cross on foot; the horses would be brought through later. All ten of us had to be blindfolded, he said.

'It's for our own good, Leif,' Garrett explained. 'There'll be disturbing sounds and sensations, but it's the things people see that send them into fits of screaming madness.'

I looked up at him and nodded. He was almost seven feet tall and dressed in chain mail from head to foot; with his two large swords at his hips, he was a formidable sight. I had been given a light chain-mail vest and a short sword, which I wore in a shoulder scabbard.

The eight other Genthai warriors ranged in age from grizzled veterans in their fifties to youths hardly older than me.

We were to cross the Barrier at night, taking our few provisions in small shoulder bags. A new moon was slowly dropping below the horizon, and I could see the Barrier ahead. The River Medie flowed towards us from its unknown source, on its banks a few stunted trees. The air was chilly.

The eyelids of the Mede were stitched shut. He was thin, his limbs like matchsticks, his face gaunt, but when he addressed us, his voice was powerful and commanding.

'In a few moments we will set off. If you want to live, you must not react to anything you hear or feel,' he told us.

Then he blindfolded us one by one – with deft, precise movements despite the fact that he could not see.

It would be the blind led by the blind – but towards what? I wondered.

We were fastened together by a long rope wrapped about our waists. Led by the Mede, we walked upstream along the riverbank. At first I was apprehensive, but all I could hear was the river chuckling over rocks. Even this sounded sinister and malevolent to my ears – like the laughter of some unseen beast delighting in our plight.

It was a cold night, and the first odd thing that I experienced was someone or something sniffing close to my face. I felt warm air on my left cheek, like the breath of someone who was inspecting me closely.

Was it the Mede? I thought suspiciously. Did they exaggerate the danger of the crossing by such tricks, seeking to increase our respect for their arcane knowledge?

Suddenly the air about me was in turmoil. I was being buffeted by a fierce wind and wondered if we had entered the Barrier itself. The series of squalls kept coming at me from different directions, and I found it hard to keep my balance.

Then, equally suddenly, all became calm and still. But, as the last fierce gust faded, I thought I heard a scream somewhere behind me. Had I imagined it?

Then I was aware of distant whisperings – and heavy footsteps close by, as if other walkers had suddenly joined our party; as if each of us had a mysterious companion.

All this unnerved me, but I took slow, deep breaths and tried to stay calm – though on several occasions my hands strayed towards my shoulder scabbard. Somehow I kept my nerve, obeying our guide's instruction.

All at once the Mede cried out, 'Halt and remove your blindfolds!'

I did as he commanded and looked about me. His voice had sounded nearby, but he was nowhere to be seen.

Two of the Genthai warriors were gone too – simply vanished into the night. These had been the last two in our column, and the rope that had bound them to us had been cut. Had one of them cried out as he was taken? Was that the noise I'd heard?

We all knew how risky the crossing could be. Now two of our party were gone, and we were down to eight. Two living, breathing men – warriors whom I had begun to count as my comrades – had been snatched away. I felt the loss keenly.

Then I looked back to see, in the faint light of the stars, the Barrier rising from Earth to heaven. It looked exactly as it had from the other side, but only now did I fully realize that we had indeed crossed over. Ahead lay the unknown lands ruled over by our enemies, the djinn.

Yet, as Konnit had told me, the landscape looked very much like the one we'd just left. The river still flowed, and there were stark, leafless trees on either bank.

We spent the day there, and the following night the Mede brought our horses through. They all came through unscathed – I was very relieved to see Laras – and we now had two spare mounts to carry our baggage. At dawn we began our journey north.

We were all fully armed. Despite my lack of skill, I carried two longswords in scabbards on Laras' flanks, along with my shield and bow. My short sword and a quiver of arrows were slung across my back.

As the river began to curve away in an easterly direction, we approached a tall tree – some sort of conifer surrounded by clumps of a silver tree fern. Garrett gestured left and we headed north, away from the river. I wondered why he'd made that sudden change of direction. All day we rode, with Garrett in the lead. Finally he called a halt, and we camped for the night.

At dawn we continued our journey, but not before Garrett had consulted what appeared to be a map.

'We have a map?' I asked him in surprise. 'Konnit said that no Genthai had ventured far beyond the Barrier.'

'Yes, Leif, we have a map. It was sketched by someone who sailed beyond the Barrier many times.'

'You mean the Trader?' I asked.

Garrett shook his head. 'Your father drew it.'

DEATH FROM THE AIR

The first ghetta will be lost in water; the second
shall bind the two unto death.

Amabramdata: the Genthai Book of Prophecy

LEIF

'Math made several journeys across the Barrier with the
Trader,' Garrett said, 'but on the last one something went
wrong. The Trader left him behind, and he returned alone
overland and drew this map of the route he took.'

'Did he quarrel with the Trader?' I asked.

Garrett shrugged. 'Nobody knows. Your father never said,
but he never worked for the Trader again. Soon after that he
bought a farm, then met and married your mother. But he
gave us this map. We will follow Math's journey in reverse.
Here – take a look.' He handed it to me.

I studied it carefully, noting the desert directly ahead, with
the forest beyond it – then two rivers that we would have to
cross. At the top, far to the north, was a city on what looked
like an island in the middle of a wide river. Just beyond that,

a thick horizontal line had been labelled *High Wall* and in that wall was marked a *Bronze Gate*.

'There's a wall and a gate marked. So my father must have gone there. I wonder how far it is. The map gives no indication of scale,' I said.

'That's where we're headed. We think it'll take us a couple of weeks,' said Garrett. 'We're hoping to take a look at that gate. Your father didn't write anything down, but it seems he said something about it when he handed over the map. From the Western Ocean he followed that river as far as the city in the Trader's ship. That wall is a big defensive structure. Our aim is to assess it – and also to see if there's any way we can get through that gate. We might decide it's better to stay on this side of the wall and defend it against whatever lies further north.'

'There must be djinn in that city . . .'

'Your father confirmed that; we want to avoid them at all costs. The truth is, Leif, we'll be lucky to cover even a small part of that distance – though verifying the accuracy of the map is of value. One day, if the route is viable, a Genthai army may follow it as they ride to do battle with the djinn.'

The sparse woods soon came to an end and the terrain became dry and featureless.

Garrett guarded the map jealously, but I'd committed much of it to memory. This area was marked as *Stony Desert*, and we were riding across coarse dark sand, rocks and scrub.

We would be visible from miles away – an easy target for the djinn. We had no idea what form they might take now, after centuries of evolution, but Ada had warned that they could look like insects or crustacea, or be similar to humans.

Whatever their shape, they would be fast and strong and would probably overwhelm us easily. I shuddered to think of hundreds, perhaps thousands, of djinn like Hob attacking us. We would surely not survive – unless, as Ada had suggested, we were able to communicate with them.

But what words could we offer in our defence? After all, we had left Midgard and crossed the Barrier in defiance of the djinn's wishes.

Garrett decided that, while we were crossing this desert, it was best to travel at night and sleep during the day, so we spent an anxious ten hours in a shallow depression, taking it in turns to keep watch. During this time there was no sign of enemy activity; indeed the only movement on that vast plain was the rippling of clumps of stunted grass in the breeze.

This was worrying: we had packed provisions for no more than a few days and were relying on hunting to supplement our diet. We'd heard wolves howling in the distance, but the Genthai didn't eat wolf meat. Even worse was the fact that there was no source of water, and our small bottles were almost empty. Moreover the grass was insufficient for the needs of our horses. We'd brought small bags of feed for them, but these wouldn't last long. The map showed that the desert would eventually give way to trees, but as there was no scale, we didn't know when that would be.

So we felt a great sense of relief when, just before dawn on the second day, the landscape began to change. The grass became greener, and soon there was the occasional tree. The following night we entered the vast pine forest promised by the map, and heard the reassuring sounds of small creatures scurrying about in the dark.

We made camp during the night, and at dawn we awoke to a chorus of birdsong. There was also a background buzz of insects, which bit us mercilessly. The air was mild again, though winter was not far off; soon there would be the first frost.

The world beyond the Barrier seemed very similar to Midgard. I was disappointed. I'd expected that as we advanced into djinn territory, the land would change.

We soon found a stream and were able to fill our bottles and water the horses. Later we set out with our bows to hunt the small grey furry animals that leaped from tree to tree. They seemed to have no fear of us and were easy prey. These creatures were quite new to us, and we risked lighting a fire to cook them.

I felt safer in the shelter of the trees. If djinn were in the vicinity, I hoped we would be difficult to detect. Moreover the glades had grass for our horses, so Garrett decided to remain there for a few days to rest, hunt and investigate our route. That first day he took one of the warriors out on a reconnaissance mission. They returned to report nothing other than a continuation of the forest. There was still no sign of djinn.

On the second day Garrett asked me to accompany him. He'd decided to range further afield: we'd ride as far as we could while the light lasted, camp for the night and return the following day.

We rode until sunset, discovering nothing new, and then made camp as planned. After supper, as we gazed into the flames, Garrett spoke without looking at me.

His words shocked me to the core.

'I don't expect to return through the Barrier, Leif,' he told me. 'I think I'll die here.'

It was a few moments before I could think of something sensible to say in reply. 'You sense your death approaching?' I asked.

He nodded. 'Yes, I have a strong sense of it. For the last four nights I've been having the same dream. It always ends in the same way.'

'Why don't you tell me about it?' I suggested.

'Maybe I will later. But I want you to do something for me. There's a woman I've been seeing from time to time. One day I hoped that we'd marry. Her name is Meira. Konnit will tell you where to find her. When you get back to the tribe, I'd like you to give this to Meira. Tell her I sent it.' He was handing me something.

I accepted it with a frown. It was a small piece of white wolf fur, clumsily stitched into a triangle.

'What is it?' I asked.

'It's called a *ghetta*. It's a love token, traditionally offered to a woman when a man asks her to marry him and joins her family. Usually it's passed from man to woman, in person, from hand to hand. But I don't expect to return. It's my way of saying goodbye and hoping that she'll remember me.'

'I'll hold onto it for you now, if it makes you feel better,' I said. 'But you'll give it to Meira yourself. I feel sure of it.'

Garrett nodded, and his mouth lifted in a smile. However, what he'd revealed made me uneasy. Garrett was the strongest and most positive of us all, the rock upon which our little expedition could rely. If he was going to die, perhaps none of us would survive.

Then I would never go home; never see Kwin again.

*

The following morning we rode back through the forest without speaking further, concentrating on the signals coming from our immediate environment and further afield; in particular, the sounds of the forest.

But it wasn't a sound that warned us something was wrong. It was the silence. The whole forest – branches, twigs, leaves, the small birds and mammals – had suddenly become perfectly still. We were the only living things moving, the only creatures making any noise. And it seemed to me that the sounds we made were increasingly loud, each hoof striking the ground like a drumstick reverberating on a taut skin.

Then, as we approached the camp, I smelled something that filled me with horror and made the bile rise in my throat. It was the metallic smell of blood and the sweet stench of rotting. Death lay ahead: I knew it.

As we rode into our camp, all my fears were confirmed. Our remaining six comrades had been slain.

I'd seen death before. I'd seen warriors and children torn to pieces by werewights; I'd seen men I cared about slain in Arena 13. But this was something else; something far beyond my experience.

At first we were wary, keeping our distance from the corpses. But we saw that pieces of flesh had been torn from the bodies with great savagery. Only their short chain-mail hauberks and helmets had resisted the attack. Their hempen trousers had gone, and hardly any flesh remained on their bones.

What could have done it? Some type of wolf? I wondered.

We paced the perimeter of the camp, looking for tracks. At last we were compelled to examine the bodies. Garrett took the lead, and I forced myself to kneel by each one in turn. I tried to hold my breath against the stench; later I tried and failed to close my ears to the sound of Garrett vomiting.

The fragments of skin and flesh that remained on the corpses had a greenish tinge. The eyes had gone, but the sockets had been fractured as if something sharp had been forced in. Small slivers of bone had broken away.

I realized that these warriors hadn't even had time to draw their weapons and, although Genthai mounts were trained to remain by their rider even if he had fallen in battle, there was no sign of the horses. Only hoof prints leading in several different directions. What had frightened them away?

I must have been in shock, not really taking in details of the scene, because it was some time before I noticed the pine needles strewn across the camp. Some even lay on the bodies.

I looked up, puzzled, then turned to Garrett and pointed out the damage to the leaf canopy. The trees above had lost most of their needles, twigs and even small branches. Garrett stared upwards, shaking his head. He looked bewildered.

I knew of no bird or flying creature that could have brought about such destruction – though it did explain why none of these men had been able to draw his weapon. The attack had been swift, possibly silent, and had come from a totally unexpected direction.

'Death came from the air!' Garrett said grimly. 'I think the djinn have found us.'

THE GREY CITY

A warrior may become a king; a king must be born
a warrior.

Amabramdata: the Genthai Book of Prophecy

LEIF

I was afraid. My fear was not for myself or for Garrett. I
feared now that we would fail to complete our quest.

As we travelled through this land, I had expected to find
enemies on every side, but its very normality had lulled me
into a false sense of safety. Now there were novel dangers, as
yet unseen. We didn't even know what we were facing.

Could our six comrades have been slain by some type of
winged djinn? I wondered. Ada had never mentioned them,
but of course they might have changed in many different ways.

The enemy could strike again at any time, and I had little
confidence that we'd fare any better than these six warriors.
Yet I didn't want to give up and go back; we'd learned little,
but I feared that Garrett would call a halt to the expedition. I
wanted to continue as far as the High Wall, the furthest
extent of my father's map.

I needn't have worried.

'We have to go on,' he said. 'But first we'll see to our dead.'

Perhaps it wasn't wise to build the funeral pyre, but that was the Genthai way and there was an ample supply of wood. Rather than waiting until sunset, as was the custom, we set light to it immediately. Garrett wanted to be well clear of the campsite before nightfall.

We watched the flames consume the bodies.

'I can't bear to think that they'll never see their families again. Never sit in the Meeting Hall again. Never go home. Their lives have been snatched away and I feel like part of me has been taken with them. I've had a vision of my own death, but I never saw this . . .' Garrett whispered.

I walked away from him and paced up and down the clearing angrily, watching the sparks fly up into the sky like souls ascending into the heavens.

Then, just before the sun went down, we rode north, still following the route indicated on my father's map. Of the mounts that had fled the clearing there was no sign.

The forest seemed without end, and progress was slow and difficult. It was with relief that, soon after dawn on the ninth day since crossing the Barrier, we saw the Grey City to our north.

It was set on a narrow plateau halfway up the slope of a high, roughly conical hill; a hill that stood at the south east of a big range of mountains. The buildings appeared to be made of grey stone, and even from a distance there was some evidence that they had fallen into disrepair.

'I'd like to take a closer look,' I told Garrett. I hoped that something new, a change from the monotony of the journey through the forest, might distract me from my morbid thoughts. I had been closer to Garrett than to the other six warriors, but now I missed them; I kept seeing their shadows among the trees, my imagination playing strange tricks on me.

'So would I, Leif, so let's do just that. If it turns out to be inhabited, we'll get as close as we can without being seen. If it's deserted, we'll investigate fully. Either way, we might learn something new about this land – and the climb will give us a good vantage point from which to spy out the lie of the land ahead. We might be able to see where the forest ends – and even as far as the High Wall and the gate.'

However, it was almost mid-afternoon before we reached the foot of the first of a series of slopes. I estimated that it would be two hours up to what I now called the Grey City, and at least another hour to descend again. That would leave us a couple of hours to explore. We should be back in the shelter of the trees by sunset, I thought, glancing nervously up at the sky.

The pine forest might have become monotonous, but even though I knew that it presented no real defence against our enemies, I'd felt better with the tree canopy above my head. Exposed to the night sky on a hillside, we would be easy targets.

So we tethered the horses and began a climb that took longer than I'd estimated. We didn't want to risk leaving our chain mail and leather armour behind, and each of us had also taken a short sword, and soon we were covered in sweat and gasping for breath in the afternoon heat. Garrett was struggling in his chain-mail hauberk.

We'd left the last scrubby bush far below and were now

scrambling over rocks and poor soil where even grasses could barely keep a precarious hold.

The city seemed as far away as ever, but it was now clear to us that it was a ruin. It wasn't as large as we'd first thought, but the buildings were densely packed, heaped one upon another in tiers that seemed to form steps designed for a giant.

Nearly three hours had passed before we reached the first dwellings. They formed a stone terrace – an apparently impenetrable wall. However, we worked our way slowly southwards until we came to a narrow archway, with steep steps leading up into near darkness.

At first they seemed to be heading directly into the build-ings, but then I saw the blue sky far above and realized that this was a narrow passageway between the houses which was easy to defend against intruders. There were no longer any guards – just a brooding silence, disturbed only by the buzz of insects and the thud of our boots on the ancient stones.

Gradually the passage began to widen and the ascent became less steep – until we emerged into a vast inner court-yard surrounded on all sides by tier upon tier of grey stone buildings.

Now we could hear the wind, moaning and whistling somewhere above, while, sheltered as we were, the air about us was still and calm. Half the courtyard was already in shadow, and fingers of darkness reached out towards us as the sun sank towards the west.

The ground here was covered in vivid green moss, but there were no other plants to be seen – probably because there was only a thin covering of soil.

Together, although neither of us had spoken, Garrett and I began to walk away from the shadows, heading for the nearest wall. Here Garrett drew a dagger from his belt and gouged a hole in the stone. The grey fell away to reveal red sandstone beneath. It seemed that the surface of each stone was covered with a crusty grey deposit.

'If we were closer to the sea, I'd say that grey powder was guano,' Garrett said.

In the far north of Midgard, near the Sea Gate, the rocky coastal regions yielded seabird excrement, which was rich in phosphates and an excellent fertilizer for the arable farms there. Deinon had an uncle who had left his small farm south of Gindeen to seek his fortune in the north; he had prospered by gathering and selling guano.

'We could be closer to the sea than we think,' I suggested.

'Not according to the chart,' said Garrett. 'And I'd smell it for sure. I've a nose for the ocean.'

'So where are the birds that deposited this?' I asked, gesturing upwards.

'For that matter, where are the windows?' Garrett asked.

I nodded. 'I wondered about that too,' I said. 'In fact, even doors are in short supply.'

All the doorways we'd seen had been blocked by slabs of stone, cut to fit perfectly.

'Why would they block them up?' Garrett wondered.

I shrugged. 'Perhaps there was a plague and they were converted into tombs. Or maybe it was a reaction to some sort of tariff. Tyron told me that, many years ago, the Protector needed to raise money and put a tax on windows in Gindeen.

Many people simply boarded up their windows and made do with less daylight.'

This didn't raise the ghost of a smile from Garrett. I reflected that it was easy to block the windows of Gindeen's wooden buildings; here the cost and effort of using stone was very different.

However, about sixty paces to the north we came upon the first open doorway. We stepped inside, and discovered that what from the outside appeared to be individual dwellings were really long communal houses. Within, there was a smell of dust and decay; the room extended into absolute darkness.

'Can you smell it?' Garrett asked, sniffing. 'The dead lie here.'

I nodded. He was right. Only bones and decay lay ahead of us. This city contained only the dead; no one had survived to honour the remains of the others. No doubt they had succumbed to some disease or plague.

I stepped outside, blinking in the brightness and drawing in a deep breath of fresh air. The light changed even as we watched, and there were new shadows on the northern wall of the courtyard. Now, for the first time, I saw steps cut into the stone, leading up the mountainside, and pointed them out to Garrett.

'Wouldn't take long,' he said, eyeing them up. 'There should be a clear view from the top. We need to see what lies ahead.'

The climb was difficult and not without danger – the steps were narrow and worn – but the view was worth it. We found ourselves on top of the highest tier of buildings, with an unbroken vista to the south, east and north.

To the south and east there was only an ocean of trees, but in the far distance, to the north, we could see a great river meandering across a plain, beyond which were faint purple hills. Long before the river, the forest gave way to grassland. That was the first of the two rivers on the map, both of which flowed from west to east.

'Another two or three days should bring us to the banks of that river,' I said. 'My father has marked a ford on the map.'

'Then let's hope the river isn't too deep,' Garrett said. 'Sometimes fords can't be crossed.'

I pointed to the east and frowned. There was a ridge of dark cloud on the horizon. 'It looks like a storm heading our way,' I said.

The big man stared at it for a while and frowned. Garrett had exceptionally good eyesight, but he shook his head. 'It's a strange-looking cloud, Leif, and I'm not sure whether it's moving towards us or heading southwest.'

It wouldn't be pleasant to be caught out on the mountainside in a storm.

At that moment the sun slipped behind a mountain, and suddenly it felt much colder. Below, in the courtyard, it looked as if night had fallen, even though there were still several hours of daylight remaining.

We began our descent almost immediately. Although I didn't speak of it to Garrett, I felt a sense of urgency: we needed to get out of this ruined place as soon as possible. There was something in the air that chilled me to the bone;

it was as if something terrible was about to happen. The warnings inside my head were shrilling an alarm.

Down in the courtyard, sheltered from the wind, it was much warmer. Once again, the air was still. Everything was silent, as if holding its breath.

It was the silence that saved us because something intruded into it; something so slight that it could barely be heard. It was a warning that sounded like the faint rustling of dried leaves. Then, as it grew louder, I realized what it was.

It was the beating of wings; the frenzied beating of thousands upon thousands of wings. Was this what our dead comrades had heard before death came from the air?

We began to run, keeping close to the wall on our left, making for the nearest open doorway. As Garrett ducked inside, I glanced behind and saw a dark, roiling cloud of winged creatures spiralling down into the courtyard from an open doorway high in the wall. They looked more like bats than birds, but I'd never seen such large bats, and there was something odd about their heads. They reminded me of insects.

Then something very strange happened: the cloud contracted and formed a distinctive shape.

It was a long curved leaf; it looked like the leaf of the silver tree fern.

It only lasted a second before that shape dissolved. Had I imagined it? I wondered.

I followed Garrett into the darkness of the building, then we headed into the utter blackness of the corridor. I was right on his heels, sensing death close behind, holding out my right hand to feel my way along the wall.

Then, suddenly, I saw Garrett's outline ahead of me. The light was coming from another door that led out into the courtyard. But then we saw a second door, almost directly opposite, half blocked by a large stone.

We stepped inside and found ourselves in a small square chamber, nothing more than a cell with that single entrance. In the dim light we saw that the stone was actually shaped like a disc.

Without the need for words, we put our shoulders to its edge.

It resisted, and I had a moment of panic. Frantically I strained to move it. I could hear Garrett groaning with effort. I was sobbing with fear, expecting to be torn into pieces at any moment.

Suddenly the stone yielded and we began to roll it across the doorway to seal ourselves in. Once set in motion, it moved more easily, guided into position by grooves in the floor and ceiling. Within seconds it had sealed off the entrance, and we waited in the utter blackness, hearing only our breaths.

But soon we heard other sounds. There was a rustling and then scratching on the other side of the stone, which rocked as if some tremendous weight was being brought to bear against it. But gradually these movements ceased and all grew quiet. Finally we settled down on the cold stone floor to rest.

It proved to be a long night and we took it in turns to sleep. In the pitch darkness it was difficult to judge the passage of time, so we waited and waited, to ensure that the morning was well advanced when we finally emerged.

Even then, rolling back the stone was fraught with danger. We hoped that those ravenous entities were creatures of the night, but we couldn't be sure. However, we couldn't stay in that cell without water or food indefinitely.

Carefully we rolled the stone back, a little at a time, pausing to listen for danger.

At last we were standing in the centre of the courtyard, feeling the sun on our heads and backs, grateful for its warmth. Wasting no time, we left the Grey City and made a rapid descent of the mountain.

Our horses were still tethered to the trees, but both were dead. A few tattered shreds of flesh and skin hung from their skeletons, but little had escaped that feeding frenzy. Even our saddlebags had been torn open and their contents devoured. However, the water bottles remained, along with our weapons.

I was stunned. Unlike the majority of Genthai warriors who, although they treated their mounts with respect, gave them little attention, I'd formed a bond with my mare. The terrible death of Laras hit me hard; strangely, it affected me just as deeply as the deaths of my companions.

'That cloud we saw in the distance – it must have been that flock of creatures,' Garrett said. 'But where are they now?'

'Maybe they're roosting somewhere in the city. Maybe they only feed at night?' I suggested.

We gathered up most of our weapons – most importantly the bows and arrows that would enable us to live off the land. However, I left behind my two longswords: they were heavy to carry, and I was more adept with my short sword and shield. So we continued our journey north, walking by day and resting by night. The nights were the worst, for I feared an attack from the sky and slept with difficulty, even when Garrett was keeping watch.

In the middle of the night I opened my eyes, feeling uneasy. Everything was silent. It was so dark that I could hardly see my hands before my face.

I listened carefully for Garrett's breathing. Nothing. It was his watch, and he was totally reliable. Surely he wouldn't have wandered off . . . I thought to call out to him softly, but even that would be dangerous. The slightest noise might attract the djinn or those flying creatures.

I rolled out from under my blanket and slowly rose onto my knees, still listening for danger. My heart sank when I heard distant sounds from the sky, somewhere above the leaf canopy.

They grew louder, and now there was no doubt: it was the beating of myriad wings.

'Garrett! Garrett!' I cried, no longer constrained by the need for silence.

Garrett didn't reply. Or maybe he did, but his answer was drowned out by the furious beating of wings that crashed through the leaves, twigs and branches to strike my body again and again.

I was paralysed. Too late, I tried to draw my sword but could not move my arm.

Then the sharp pains began: it was as if needles were being thrust deep into my eyes, my belly, my arms and my legs. Sharp beaks pierced my body and tore pieces of my flesh away. I would have done anything to escape that pain. I cried out for death to take me.

Then there was silence, and I felt myself being shaken gently, Garrett's voice softly calling my name. I opened my eyes and, with a feeling of intense relief, realized that it had just been one of the recurrent nightmares that had been troubling me since we'd crossed the Barrier.

I sat up, sweat pouring from me, and Garrett patted me on the back in sympathy, for I'd told him about the nightmares.

'Another bad dream, Leif? The same one?'

'Yes, it's always the same one.'

I knew that Garrett had nightmares too. So far, he hadn't told me about his – the one that ended with his death. I knew he would do so when he was ready.

'If they do come for us in the dark, the best we can hope for is to kill one each. If I prove to be too slow,' Garrett said with a smile, 'you'll have to kill two. Don't let me down.'

DEATH

In the vision, the girl wears red boots. There is
arterial blood splattered at her feet.

It may be her own.

Amabramdata: the Genthai Book of Prophecy

KWIN

I opened my eyes and, with a pang, remembered that Leif
was no longer here. He'd already been gone for over a month
and I was missing him.

Part of me had wanted to ask him not to go, but I knew
that would be a mistake. The expedition beyond the Barrier
would go ahead with or without him, and if he'd given up
his place, he would have regretted it for the rest of his life.
I knew he was proud to have been chosen and believed
that he would learn things that might help us to destroy
Hob.

Then I remembered that today was my birthday, which
made me both happy and sad.

I was happy to be seventeen – a year closer to being an
adult, when I hoped my father would stop treating me like a

child. I wanted to be given the same respect as he accorded Ada and Teena. Eighteen would be the age of my maturity; then he could no longer deny me that. It was just one year away!

Yet my birthday was always a sad occasion too. My mother had died on my first birthday. I tried to picture her face. My father said that I had her looks. I didn't remember her, but she lived on in my mind because of the stories he had told me and Teena when we were children.

I dressed quickly and sat facing the mirror, looking first at the number 13 that I'd had tattooed on my forehead. Years ago, long before my father's time, combatants fighting in Arena 13 had done this as a badge of pride, a sign of what they were to show the world.

The clasp on my father's belt had the same insignia, but he'd never dream of marking his face. He'd certainly been shocked when he first saw my forehead!

I stared at the girl in the mirror, and then asked the usual question:

'Girl in the mirror on the wall,
Who is the fastest of them all?'

I watched her mouth move as, together, we spoke the answer:

'Kwin!'

It was part of the longer ritual I went through before combat to steady my nerves and reinforce my self-belief.

Then I went downstairs to breakfast.

Ada was already there; she came over and gave me a hug. 'Happy birthday, Kwin,' she said with a smile as she handed me a parcel. 'Open it later – if you don't like it, don't be afraid to tell me. We can go back to the shop together and exchange it for something else.'

I returned her smile. 'Thank you, Ada. I'm sure it'll be perfect.'

I looked at her. She had seemed a lot happier recently. I knew that she still missed her husband, Tal, slain by Hob in the arena. She still looked no older than her early thirties. I had heard tales of other twice-born who had been bought from the Trader, their souls clothed in false flesh. At least one had aged rapidly and died within a year. So far Ada seemed to be in the best of health and still retained her youth.

At that moment my father and sister appeared. They were both carrying presents, but his was very small indeed. I wondered what it contained.

My father was starting to show his age, and that made me sad. I wanted him to remain strong and in his prime, but one day he would be an old man. The lines on his face were more pronounced, but what made it worse was the sadness in his eyes. After all these years he still missed my mother, and the anniversary of her death was always a melancholy occasion. She'd fallen victim to the autumn flu that had swept through Gindeen, killing hundreds of its citizens.

'Happy birthday, Kwin,' my father said, kissing me on both cheeks before giving me a quick hug. Then he handed me that small parcel. 'It's something that belonged to your mother . . .'

I began to open it, but he shook his head and put his hand on mine to stop me. 'Open it later, in the privacy of your room, and please wear it tonight for your party.'

I thanked him, and then gave Teena a hug and thanked her for her present, which I also kept for later. Then we sat down to breakfast with Teena's young son, Robbie. He was a fair-haired, pale, unhappy-looking toddler. As usual, I did my best to cheer him up, but was rewarded with only a slight smile.

I wasn't looking forward to my party – I didn't like the fuss – but I hadn't the heart to complain because it made my father happy. Besides, it would only be a few family members and close colleagues.

Before going to work I went up to my room to open my presents. To my delight, I discovered that Ada had bought me a pair of Trigladius blades to use in the arena. The handles were ornate and the blades perfectly balanced. They must have cost her a fortune. I hadn't yet opened my other presents, but surely this had to be the best of the three – not that I would ever say that to anyone!

I opened Teena's present next: she had meant well, but it wasn't something I would have chosen. It was a long maroon dress with white lace on the collar and hem – no doubt she expected me to wear it for the party. I did wear dresses, but I preferred them short and tight to suit my body which, though I say so myself, was honed to perfection. I didn't work to keep it that way out of vanity. I carried not an ounce of fat, and every muscle was developed to serve me in Arena 13.

Teena had never recovered from the death of her husband, Kern, who'd also been slain by Hob in the arena. She was still fragile, and I didn't want to cause her pain. Tonight I would grit my teeth and wear that dress for her sake.

Finally I opened my father's present. It was a single

earring, beautifully wrought from silver alloy in the shape of a tiny white wolf. There was a note with it:

I gave this to your mother, Jacanda, many years ago, on the day we were married, as a token of our love. There was a pair, but the other is lost and this is all that remains. Please wear it.
With love,
Your father, Tyron

My earlobes were pierced, but I rarely wore jewellery. For this I would make an exception. I fitted it carefully into my left ear where my hair was cut short to reveal my scar. Then I studied my face in the mirror. The little wolf gleamed in the late autumn sunshine that streamed almost horizontally through the windows.

I'd been wrong. It was even better than the blades.

I would wear it always.

I walked across the city towards the admin building. My father was the most successful artificer in Gindeen, with the largest stable of human combatants and lacs. That often made for a hard morning's work, which could occasionally spill over to take up a large chunk of my afternoon. But this was the lull between seasons when no fighting took place in the Wheel.

It wouldn't be too bad, I thought – just a couple of tedious hours of paperwork which, today, would include dealing with the wages. Then I would be able to return home for some combat practice.

The admin building was a large oblong wooden structure, two storeys high. The outside was painted grey, which matched the boring tasks that went on inside. My heart sank as I approached it. It sank even further when I saw who was waiting for me.

It was Jon, who'd been my boyfriend before Leif.

Jon was good-looking and I'd once been crazy about him. But all that was in the past. Now I was with Leif; I never even looked twice at another boy. Unfortunately Jon still thought he could win me back.

As I drew nearer, I saw that he was carrying a parcel.

'Happy birthday, Kwin! Here's your present,' he said.

I hesitated. To refuse would gain me nothing. I didn't want to encourage him; nor did I want to hurt or offend him in any way.

'That's new,' he said, staring at my earring. 'Is that a present from Leif?'

I shook my head. Leif hadn't given me a present before he left for the Barrier. I'd been slightly hurt – after all, he'd known that my birthday was just a few weeks away. But I didn't really blame him: he'd been so caught up in his preparations to leave. Maybe he'd remember when he returned. In any case, last year he'd bought me the best present ever – a pair of red Trig boots for fighting in Arena 13.

'No, it's from my father,' I replied.

'What did Leif buy you?' Jon persisted.

'I'm sorry, Jon, but I have to go. I've a lot to do today.'

'If he doesn't come back, Kwin, I want you to know that I'll still be here for you.'

'He'll be back, Jon, you can be sure of that!' I snapped angrily before pushing past him to enter the building, ignoring the proffered parcel.

I used my anger to fuel my work. Never had I completed the accounts and wages so quickly. Then it was back home for an energetic workout on the training floor my father had installed. In size and shape, it was an exact replica of Arena 13.

I was working with a new lac that Ada had patterned for me, and there was a lot to do. I spent most of the afternoon dancing behind it and developing Ulum – the sound-code that would enable us to communicate while fighting – while Ada looked on. You communicated with your lac by drumming on the floor with your boots. This told it what position to take up and what manoeuvre to execute. It was a private code, unique to each combatant and lac – your opponent couldn't understand it.

Finally I danced in front of the lac in attack mode, trying to work off the anger that was still simmering inside me. I knew that it wasn't Leif's fault – his mission was important – but circumstances had taken him from me. It had happened so quickly that he hadn't thought about my birthday.

The afternoon went well, and Ada was pleased with what she saw, but at last she called a halt.

'That's enough for today, Kwin. Time to get ready for your party!'

I pulled a face – though I knew she was right. I wanted to look my best for the sake of my father and sister, so I went to wash and change into Teena's dress.

I don't remember much about the party. I still felt angry, but I had to put on a smile and appear cheerful. Maybe I drank too much punch – or perhaps it was stronger than usual; whatever the reason, the evening flew by quickly. I remember dancing with a young man I'd been introduced to for the first time – he and his parents were surprise guests at the party. His name was Goodwin and he paid me a lot of attention.

After the party my father took me up to his study. That was something that happened only rarely, and I knew he had something important to say. I wondered whether I'd made a fool of myself at the party and he was about to tell me off.

I sat down facing him across the desk. Then he gave me a warm smile, and I knew that I wasn't in trouble. As usual, my father was sipping his glass of red wine.

'You seemed to be enjoying yourself tonight,' he said.

'It was fun. Thanks for the party – and thanks again for giving me the earring,' I said, touching it.

'The young man you danced with . . .'

'You mean Goodwin?' I asked. Although I'd mostly been with Goodwin, I'd also danced with one of Wode's sons.

'Yes, young Goodwin. His parents have just made a formal proposal of betrothal. He's their eldest son. They came to the party tonight to appraise you and our family. They liked what they saw.'

I was stunned. Some of the wealthier families in Gindeen still believed in arranged marriages. It was a way of consolidating wealth: the eldest son inherited most of this; added to the bride's dowry, it ensured continuity of social standing.

'I refuse!' I said, coming to my feet, feeling my face burn with anger.

'Of course you do. Please sit down, Daughter, and listen to the rest of what I have to say,' he said calmly.

I sat down and took a deep breath, trying to control my

anger. 'I love Leif. One day I hope we'll be married!' I told him.

'I know that – one day I'll be happy to stand at your side and give you both my blessing. All I ask is that you follow the niceties with Goodwin. You've met him now. You need only be in his company twice more, and then we can refuse him. Why upset him? His parents are good people – he'll eventually make someone an excellent husband—'

'Not me!' I snapped.

'Of course it won't be you, Kwin. But why cause offence? Next week his parents will hold a party and we will be invited. The following week there will be a third party on neutral ground. All you have to do is dance with Goodwin and make conversation. You seemed to find it pleasant enough tonight. Then we can make a polite formal refusal. Won't you do that for me?'

I found it hard to say no. Goodwin's father was the joint owner of one of the largest gambling houses. In order to unite the city and cement the alliance with the Genthai, Tyron needed to keep such men on his side.

I sighed and nodded. I'd agreed, but it wasn't the best end to my birthday.

THE STONE BRIDGE

And they came at last to the second river, and saw
that the chart was good. And here they saw a
wonder indeed – a bridge built of stone.

Not without justification was this later named
the Bridge of Sorrows.

The History of the Conflict by Eitel the Pessimist

LEIF

Now that we had to travel on foot, it took us almost three
days to reach the river we'd seen from the heights above the
Grey City.

There was no bridge, but it was wide and shallow; in places
the water reached no higher than our ankles, and fording it
proved easy. Once across, we continued our journey north.
We entered a second pine forest, but this time the terrain
was hilly, our progress impeded by deep, treacherous ravines
that ran from east to west, and many days were wasted in
backtracking to find a way round. The map hadn't been
drawn to scale, so it didn't show a clear way through.

Each night, just before sunset, we halted, and Garrett

dutifully amended the chart, trying to add detail to what had previously shown only major features. Each ravine was recorded, and the fastest and most direct route northwards clearly marked.

The chart had shown mountains and the Grey City, and next to the latter Garrett drew a skull as a warning, aware that those who followed needed to avoid it.

Finally, through the trees, we glimpsed the second river marked on the map, and here the chart seemed to be accurate.

Another week on foot, I thought, should bring us to the city on the island, and the High Wall beyond it.

From the wooded slope, I looked down at the river, now less than a day away. Below were grasslands dotted with broad-leaved, deciduous trees and scrub. We were about to leave the shelter of the pine forest and would be more vulnerable to attack from the sky.

The sun was setting and the shadows were lengthening down in the valley. I'd previously noticed what I took to be a ford across the river – an area of shallow water with stones close to the surface. But now it was clearer, and I could see that it was the bridge marked on my father's map. I pointed it out to Garrett.

'I can see it!' he cried. 'No need to get our feet wet this time.'

We moved on towards the river, taking the path of least resistance through the trees and scrub.

Less than twenty-four hours later we were standing on the banks of that river, marvelling at the bridge, which was still some way downstream.

The river was a wide, surging torrent, its far bank dauntingly distant. Never had I seen such a river. By comparison, the puny ones of Midgard were hardly more than muddy streams. But the greater miracle was the bridge; the stone bridge that spanned the torrent in thirteen long, graceful, sweeping arches. The map had given no indication of its magnificence.

Midgard had only single-span bridges made of wood and rope that needed constant renewal. This looked as if it had existed for centuries and might endure until the end of time itself.

'How would you build such a bridge?' I asked. 'How could you even begin?'

The stone supports went right down into the river bed. What kind of technology could have held the water at bay while the masons worked? I wondered.

We made camp right on the riverbank, but at some distance from the bridge. Until now we'd seen no sign of djinn activity but, had there been humans in the vicinity, the bridge would doubtless have been part of a trading route.

When the sun set, Garrett slept while I stood watch. The time passed uneventfully, and soon it was my turn. At first my sleep was peaceful, but then, once again in my dream I heard the beating of wings. This time there was more than just darkness, with the tree canopy overhead. I was back in the central courtyard of the Grey City, turning to watch the winged creatures swarming down from the open doorway high in the wall. Time seemed to halt. That moment became an eternity, and my terror had gone so that I was able to study them with detachment.

It was hard to estimate their size – they were too far away – but it was now clear that they were shaped like insects, with three distinct body parts that gleamed silver, like highly polished armour. But there was something very strange about their heads. Something disturbing, I thought . . . But they were just too far away to see clearly.

Suddenly they formed a pattern in the sky: the image of the silver tree fern.

Then I woke up; Garrett was shaking me. Over his shoulder I could see the grey clouds to the east tinged with pink. It was almost dawn.

I sat up. 'Why didn't you wake me?' I asked.

'I knew I wouldn't be able to sleep again, but you were tired,' Garrett said. 'You'd have done the same for me. Here's breakfast . . .'

I sat up and accepted a strip of cold meat, chewing it without enthusiasm. We couldn't risk lighting a fire. Anything might lie in wait across that bridge.

'I heard noises in the night,' Garrett told me, 'from somewhere near the central span. It sounded like a woman weeping. And look at that!'

He pointed at the bridge. In the grey pre-dawn light, dark birds could be seen wheeling high above it. My heart skipped a beat, but then I saw that they bore no resemblance to the winged creatures that brought death from the sky. They were too far away for me to be sure, but they reminded me of the vultures that soared above the slaughterhouse and the Wheel back in Gindeen.

'It looks like we've an eventful morning ahead. Let's make a start,' I suggested.

I began to rise, but Garrett put a hand on my arm. 'I think we should go back,' he said. 'Head back towards the Barrier.'

I looked at him in amazement. 'Go back? Why?'

'We've come a long way and seen a lot, Leif – much more than I expected. We've reached the second river. We've identified a threat from the air and know that it's located near that ruined city. We should take that knowledge back with us – take it back while we can.'

I looked up at him searchingly, but he had turned his head away. 'You think something's going to happen, don't you? Is it the bridge?'

Garrett nodded and gestured towards the river. 'If I try to cross it, I'll die. I saw that stone bridge in my dreams. I die on that bridge.'

'Then *you* go back, Garrett. Take what we've learned with you. You'll save lives by doing so. But I need to go on. There's more to see, and I intend to go all the way. I'm going to follow my father's map to its very end. I want to see the High Wall and the gate – and find out if we can get through it. I want to take that knowledge back to the Genthai. If they ride through the Barrier, they need as much information as possible.'

A silence fell between us. I took a long drink from my water bottle and stared out across the river. The turbulence of the previous day had abated, and now, although there was a current, the water lapped at the banks with a soothing rhythm. However, it did look very deep.

Garrett turned towards me again. 'It's not because I'm afraid,' he said. 'But if I die now, I'll miss something I've waited a lifetime for. When that army of Genthai warriors rides across the bridge to attack the djinn, I want to be with them.'

'Then you deserve to be with them. Go back.'

Garrett frowned and then shook his head. 'No. Give me the ghetta!' he demanded.

I sighed, retrieved the small piece of white wolf fur from my jacket and held it out. I suddenly realized what Garrett intended, but there was nothing I could do. He seized the love token and tossed it into the river. It was carried away by the current, and then sank.

'I wanted to shame her,' he said. 'I hoped that Meira would be hurt when it was sent to her after my death. You see, she's already refused me three times. When I persisted, she called me an oaf. But now it doesn't matter any more. Who could blame her anyway? A man like me isn't meant to marry.'

Garrett came to his feet and began to strap the longsword and shield across his back, looking with determination at the bridge. 'A warrior doesn't need a woman,' he said, without a trace of bitterness in his voice. 'Maybe I'll never ride across that bridge with the army, but I'll die bravely now. Let's go. Remember me, Leif. If you do get back safely, then tell them what I did.'

My heart was heavy as we prepared to leave: Garrett had infected me with his sense of foreboding. Perhaps we'd both die on that bridge ... I wondered if I'd ever see Kwin again.

Soon we were walking across it. Up close, it was even more impressive – so wide that five or six men could have walked abreast – but at the point where each span met, it narrowed considerably: only a single horse could have passed through the gap in comfort.

One day a Genthai army might indeed ride across this bridge, but they'd be forced to do so in single file, and any supply wagons would either have to be left behind or dismantled and carried across.

Beneath our feet was a mosaic of grey, blue and red tiles; at our sides parapets lined the bridge; on top of them, every twenty paces or so, were lifelike carvings of the heads of predatory animals or birds. At the midpoint of the first span there were two black metal spikes. I wondered what their purpose could be.

I stared at the central span ahead of us, where the vultures were still circling. Even as I watched, three of the birds swooped down towards the bridge. The sun was now just above the horizon, like a baleful red eye peering through the ribbed clouds, turning the waters of the river to blood. In the dim light I thought I saw a number of figures crouching beside the left-hand parapet.

'There, Garrett – what do you see? There – just below those birds.'

'Humans,' Garrett answered. 'Five in all. Three of them are children. They seem to be tied to the bridge.'

I was astounded by his reply. The only humans left alive were supposed to be confined within the Barrier. This contradicted everything the people of Midgard believed. What did it mean? Had the djinn done this?

We broke into a run; as we neared the central span, we came to a halt, shocked to see the butchery that had been carried out here. On our right, by the eastern parapet, were three male corpses. They'd been stripped naked and partially dismembered. Above them on the wall there were seven spikes, and three carried severed heads, the faces and beards covered in red gore.

Two vultures were feeding on the corpses, their neck feathers streaked with blood. A third was pecking at the furthest of the three heads.

Garrett ran at them, and they flapped up into the air and began to circle menacingly.

I turned to the western parapet: the seven spikes were empty, but tied to iron rings set in the base of that low wall lay two pale-skinned women with golden hair. I could see no wounds to their bodies, which were clad in rags, but their hair was matted with blood.

Most pitiful of all were the three children, not one of them more than two years old. They cowered beside their mothers and began to scream hysterically as I approached.

The women made no sound at all, but stared at me with wide eyes as if their wits had fled. I knelt and drew my knife, cutting the ropes that bound their arms and legs.

They made no attempt to move, so I seized one of the women by the hand and pulled her gently to her feet. She stood there uncertainly.

The second woman was harder to lift; the moment she was on her feet she began to shake, and the children wailed even more loudly.

But not loud enough to drown out the sudden sound that came from the north bank of the river: it was the harsh threatening blare of a brass horn.

Garrett was now pointing at the furthest span, where the

bridge met the distant bank. 'Warriors!' he cried. 'They're coming this way!'

I picked up one of the children and seized the arm of the nearer of the two women. 'Come on!' I shouted, and began to guide her towards the southern bank. The other woman began to hobble after us. Garrett picked up the remaining two children and carried them, one under each arm.

We'd hardly reached the next span when I saw figures pursuing us and shouting. At this rate we'd be overtaken long before we reached the bank. I released the woman's arm and thrust the child into her arms. She stood there, cringing, as if expecting to receive a blow.

I tried to smile at her, but in truth it was more of a grimace.

'That way!' I shouted, pointing towards the bank. 'Go on!'

She didn't move, so I gave her a gentle push. But then Garrett was roaring and shouting and waving his arms at them all like a wild, demented giant. The women and their children recoiled at the sight, and at last began to retreat.

Together Garrett and I turned to face the approaching threat. He drew his longsword and glanced right and left, as if gauging the width from parapet to parapet. He gave a few swings with it and grunted in satisfaction.

'How many are there?' I asked.

'Only nine,' Garrett said, 'so hardly worth the sharing. Let's make it six for me and three for you.'

I unslung my bow, quiver, shield and short sword, setting the first two down close to the parapet. Then I hefted the sword and shield, attempting some practice swings.

'First strike is mine,' Garrett said. 'Brawn before speed!'

I nodded, then stepped back, allowing him plenty of space to meet the first of our foes.

The longsword was more usually used from horseback, and the warrior elite carried two, one in each hand. On foot, it was a far more awkward weapon, and much depended upon rhythm, on using the weight of the sword like a pendulum. But Garrett was an expert with the weapon, and big and strong enough to wield it with devastating effect.

I watched the first warrior running towards Garrett; close to his side he held a spear with a barbed blade. His skin was very pale and he was dressed in skins decorated with animal skulls; his golden hair – the same colour as that of the women – hung in long braids threaded with what appeared to be teeth.

He was passing through a narrow section, with two others close behind. It was only as they emerged that I realized all three were actually sharing the same long spear, holding it like a battering ram.

The force of their combined weight against the massed ranks of an enemy would be formidable, but against the longsword of Garrett it was madness. He simply stepped aside and swung the sword with such force that it took the first man's head clean off his body, the blade burying itself deep in the chest of the second.

The third released the spear shaft and stumbled to his knees, reaching for the axe at his side, so I stepped forward and despatched him with a swift stabbing blow to the throat. Garrett was still tugging his sword from the body of the second man, so I went forward to meet the next attack.

I waited with my legs slightly apart, balanced on the balls

of my feet, my shield held high to protect my head. The warrior in the lead threw an axe at me. It spun over and over, and I deflected it easily. It soared over the parapet and I heard the splash as it hit the water.

Then, fighting my instincts, I whirled right, in amongst our attackers, splitting the first man's forehead open with the sharp edge of my shield and killing another with a short chopping blow to the neck.

Both men cried out, but I still heard Garrett's urgent shout of 'Down!' and immediately dropped to my knees – just in time to see the longsword flash in a murderous arc through the space where, only a second earlier, my own head had been.

Within seconds it was all over. Three times the blade of Garrett followed its deadly arc and, when I came to my feet, our enemies were all dead or dying.

But then, once again, we heard the blare of a horn from the far bank. Garrett turned and gazed into the distance, then shook his head. 'There are too many of them,' he said. 'You go. I'll hold them off as long as I can.'

I shook my head. 'We'll fight together,' I insisted.

Garrett placed his longsword on the tiles at his feet and unslung the round shield from his back. 'I'll fight there,' he said, pointing to the place where the parapets drew close together. 'Only one can get to me at a time. But you go – there's no choice. One of us has to return or our journey's been for nothing.'

What Garrett said made sense, but I couldn't bring myself to abandon him. I could see the enemy warriors racing towards us. After twenty I stopped counting. There were at least thirty of them. We were hopelessly outnumbered. If I stayed, we'd both die.

'Then let *me* do it. I'll hold them while you go,' I said, trying one last time, but knowing that my words were wasted.

'I dreamed this,' cried Garrett. 'I die here on this bridge. Even if I run, I'll die before I reach the bank. At least you have a chance. Go now, before it's too late! Take the map.'

He held it out, and I thrust it into the front of my shirt, and then turned to look at the enemy.

The first man was approaching the place where the bridge narrowed; Garrett lifted his short sword and shield, and stepped forward to meet him. There was the clash of metal upon metal; then a duller sound – that of a blade penetrating cloth, flesh and bone.

I turned and, leaving my bow and quiver behind but holding my shield and sword, began to run towards the southern bank. Ahead, the two women seemed to have halted on the edge of the bridge. Then, to my dismay, I realized that there were enemies on both banks – enemies that had perhaps watched us for some time, waiting until we were trapped at the centre of the bridge. But then I saw that these warriors, who gathered in a semicircle round the women, were darker-skinned and wore armour made of blue metal rings.

Then a blade flashed red in the morning sunlight, and I heard a woman scream. I increased my speed. There were four – maybe five of them. Not too many if I went in hard and fast.

One of them was holding a child up by its leg. I heard one of the women begin to shout, letting out a babble of words.

They were wasted. The child was tossed in a high arc into

the water. The woman screamed, her voice high and thin; she sounded on the verge of insanity. The scream was cut off very suddenly, and then the two remaining children were thrown into the water, to be carried away by the current.

The warriors had been too busy with their butchery to notice me. Maybe it hadn't been a trap after all. I suddenly realized that these men were different to the ones we had fought on the bridge. Those on the northern bank had been trying to rescue their women and children; we had prevented them, and even driven the prisoners towards their blue-clad enemies.

I saw the surprise on these other men's faces as I lunged right and left with shield and sword. Then I was past them, running up the slope towards a small grove of trees. Let them follow me. I'd welcome it after what they'd done. They were killers of women and children. There were only three left now – I'd pick them off one at a time. The fastest would die first.

The trees grew in a circle. No sooner had I entered the copse than I came to a sudden halt, astonished at what I saw.

There were five people there – four men and a woman. The men were tall, slim and dark-skinned, also dressed in that strange blue armour. Their noses were hooked and prominent, and their faces were all identical. The men flanked the woman, two on each side.

The woman was mounted on a creature unlike anything I'd ever seen before. It was similar in size to a horse, but its legs were thicker and it was almost twice as long. The wild boar might have been a distant cousin: it had a flat snout and sharp tusks that curved upwards, though its eyes looked almost human; they regarded me with a mixture of interest and malevolence. Its body was rounded, but muscles rippled beneath its grey hide, and upon its broad back, on a raised seat crafted from red leather, sat the woman, who stared at me with imperious eyes.

Fascinated, I lowered my sword and shield and studied her. She looked young, hardly out of her teens, but the expression on her face spoke of authority and purpose. Her skin was an astonishing pale green colour, but when I looked at her mouth – remembering tales of mythical creatures beyond the Barrier who were said to need no food, being able to absorb energy directly from the sun – I saw two rows of perfectly formed white teeth, while her lips were painted black – like those of the women in the gallery in Arena 13. Her long black hair was tied back. The belt tied around a dress of simple white cotton bore two ornamental daggers, each handle fashioned to resemble a ram's head. And at her neck was a narrow black torc studded with small rubies.

Then I noticed the small tattoo on her forehead. It was the leaf of a silver tree fern. It brought back a vivid memory of the formation of the flying creatures.

I suddenly felt dizzy – hardly aware of what I was doing. All thoughts of what had just happened had been erased from my memory.

As if in a dream, I lifted my sword in salute and returned it to its scabbard.

The woman's mouth smiled at me, but her expression was condescending. Then she extended her arm so that her forefinger was pointing directly at me. A purple spark left the tip and surged towards me.

Then I felt my heart lurch and stop; there was a sudden choking sensation in my throat, and I felt myself falling . . .

When I opened my eyes again, I was standing near the river, beside the woman and the strange creature she rode. My whole body was shaking and I felt cold. I looked down and saw that I was naked. They'd taken everything from me – my weapons, my chain-mail shirt, clothes and boots.

My memory had come back, and I remembered the map, and was suddenly filled with despair. They'd taken that too. Had all our struggles been for nothing? Had poor Garrett died in vain?

I noticed that my wrists were chained and fastened to the creature's saddle. Another chain went around my neck, which was being pulled taut from behind, keeping me away from the beast, drawing the other two chains to their full extent.

When I tried to see who was pulling it, I felt something sharp jab me between the shoulder blades and a hot pain shot down my spine – a pain out of all proportion to the force used. It made me gasp and turn away immediately, but not before I'd glimpsed the dark blue chain mail worn by the woman's attendants. All four were no doubt somewhere behind me.

The woman turned in her seat and looked down at me, and for the first time I saw the cruelty in her eyes.

The beast began to lumber towards the bridge and I was forced to follow, staggering along behind it. As it waddled along, I glanced to my left and saw a circle of pale-faced warriors standing close to the river. They were dressed like those we'd fought earlier, but their expressions were sullen and defiant. But then the woman looked down at them and, as one, they knelt on the grass and bowed low until their foreheads touched the ground.

We headed across the bridge; when we reached a section where it narrowed, the creature's hide scraped against the stone.

When we reached the central span, to my horror and dismay I saw that Garrett's head had been stuck on a spike on the parapet. I began to weep, and the woman turned in her saddle and gazed at me again with that cruel smile.

I thought of Garrett: he had dreamed of his death, and that dream had come to pass. He would never ride with a Genthai army. However, I would ensure that his memory lived on; that he hadn't died in vain. My father's map might be gone, but I still remembered what it showed. And I resolved to add new details whenever possible. Above all, I was now determined to live. I would survive and return to Midgard with knowledge that would ensure our victory.

Suddenly I was filled with new resolve, and my despair lifted. There was much to learn here, I thought. The warriors we'd fought on the bridge seemed hardly more than barbarians; they would pose no threat to a mounted Genthai army. But the blue-armoured people were a different proposition. What power had the woman used to make me lose consciousness? I wondered. What was its source?

Judging by those who now held me captive, not all who dwelt beyond the Barrier were equally powerful.

It was vital that I learn the extent of the threat they posed.

I had to escape and take that knowledge home.

LEIF THE SCHOLAR

The student must teach and the teacher must learn.
Only through that comes true knowledge.
The History of the Conflict by Eitel the Pessimist

LEIF

On the day following my capture, directly north of the river I was left with a small tribe of the blond-haired people we'd fought on the bridge. At first I thought I'd been handed over to be killed. Then, later, when they fed me generously, I thought slavery would be my fate.

I tried to be cooperative: I wanted to live, and to see Kwin again. How terrible it would be to die so far from home, so far from those I cared about.

However, I was fed well and given exercise, but enough rest to allow my feet to heal – walking without boots had given me blisters – although rarely released from my chains unless under close guard. My captors made no attempt to communicate with me. There were perhaps a couple of hundred in the tribe, living in caves and stone shelters in the lee of the low, rocky hills. They kept pigs and hunted daily; meat was the staple diet.

As the days passed and I settled into a routine, my spirits sank. I missed Garrett, and in my nightmares I saw his head on that spike. I thought only of escape. Reaching the High Wall seemed a hopeless task; I just wanted to return home with the knowledge I had.

My captors had given me skins to wear, but one morning they took me outside into the cold and stripped those clothes from me, driving me at spear-point into the forest. Once again it seemed as if I was facing death.

But then, ahead of me, I saw the woman sitting on the great beast, accompanied by the same four identical warriors in blue armour. Once more I was chained to the beast and we headed north.

Towards dusk we emerged from the trees and descended onto an arid plain which had not been marked on my father's map. Its pale red dust was strewn with fragments of flint, and at its centre stood a saucer-shaped, rocky platform, bronze in colour, and embedded with myriad fragments of crystal, which glittered in the light of the dying sun.

As we approached, I made out thin, twisted spires, and at first I thought we were approaching a citadel like Hob's. But then I saw that this was much smaller, little more than a roughly circular elevation supporting a number of crooked towers that reminded me of termite mounds. The whole structure seemed to have been shaped by something other than human hands.

My chains were removed and I was prodded at spear-point towards a narrow opening – a dark vertical crack in the rock wall. As I entered, I looked at the woman, but she was staring up at the largest of the towers. Two of the blue-clad warriors stood in attendance on either side of the beast, while the remaining two escorted me inside.

I found myself in a dark, narrow passageway that led steeply down. There was some light, but it was impossible to detect its source and I was immediately aware of a humid warmth, which was welcome after the chill outside. It felt like a summer night, with a pleasant breeze.

I was also aware of sounds that were almost musical; it was as if they were linked to the breeze, even caused by the circulation of air. They rose and fell, a symphony of cries and wails and sighs, all tinged with sadness. I felt a sudden pain as I remembered Garrett, who had died so bravely.

Down and down we went, a spear-point never far from my back, until at last we entered a vast circular chamber. There were metal doors set around it; the nearest of these was opened and I was prodded inside, the door clanging shut behind me.

I heard the footsteps of my two captors receding, so I examined the door, but it had no handle on my side. I traced its cool metal edge with my fingers, but it fitted tightly against the wall and there was no way to get it open.

I turned and peered into the interior of my cell. Slowly my eyes adjusted to the gloom and I discovered that it wasn't a cell at all but a narrow passageway like the one I'd followed earlier. This also led steeply downwards, and I stepped along warily until it opened out into a large square chamber, almost as big as the circular one I'd just left. It had no windows and, again, no visible source of illumination, but there was enough light to see by – though what I saw filled me with disquiet.

Set high in each of the four walls were metal rings, slightly thicker than a human forearm; at the very centre of the floor was a circular opening.

I approached this carefully, knelt at its edge and peered down. I saw stone steps spiralling down into the darkness, and a sudden irrational fear began to overpower me at the thought of what might be waiting there. My terror was that of a child stuck in a nightmare where all courage has fled and there is only the desperate need to awake.

I knew I should force myself to make the descent, but a wise voice in my ear counselled caution. I should rest first.

I moved away from the opening and approached the far wall. Once again my legs trembled in fear, for now I could see another hole in the floor – a long and narrow pit running the whole length of that wall.

I peered over, but could see only darkness; however, I sensed, hidden within it, something looking up at me. I quickly pulled back.

My eyes gradually adjusted to the gloom and, for the first time, I saw a shallow recess in the wall to my left. Inside was a pallet with a single blanket so, feeling utterly weary and suddenly indifferent to the dangers that might be lurking below, I lay down and covered myself with the blanket.

I lay there thinking of Garrett. Then my thoughts turned to home and Kwin, and I remembered the last hours we had spent together. I tried to visualize her face: I could see the 13 tattooed on her forehead; the hair, shorter on one side; and her scar. But her face seemed to shimmer and, as I drifted closer to sleep, for some reason it changed into the face of the cruel woman who had pointed her finger at me, causing me to fall unconscious.

Eventually, overcome by weariness, I fell asleep.

I awoke slowly, aware of the need to relieve my bladder. However, I was warm and comfortable, so I kept drifting in and out of sleep, until at last I pulled off the blanket and opened my eyes.

Instantly I came to my feet.

The chamber had been transformed: torches were suspended from the metal rings, and it now blazed with a yellow, flickering light. A small table covered with a green cloth had been set by the circular hole in the floor. Upon it lay dishes of meat and fruit, along with a bronze decanter filled with liquid; beside it stood two crystal goblets and a number of smaller, ornate pewter cups decorated with representations of birds.

I was hungry, but first I needed to urinate: I looked around, quickly deciding that the narrow passage leading to the door was the furthest point from my bed and the table. It was then that I saw a second recess in the opposite wall and went to investigate.

It contained a small circular hole in the floor to the left and a larger oblong depression to the right. I urinated into the hole, and then quickly returned to the table and picked up a plate of some pale meat. I sniffed it suspiciously, but it smelled fine.

Anyway, why should my captors bother to poison me? I reflected. Had they wanted me dead, they would surely have slain me before now.

I ate quickly; the meat was delicious – peppery and pungent so that it was difficult to identify the type of creature it came from. Next I tried a round orange fruit and found this to be sweet and juicy, but also alien to anything I'd ever tasted before.

Then, as I was about to pour myself a drink, I heard a sound from below – the echo of distant footsteps growing steadily louder. They had a hard edge, as if metal was rhythmically striking stone.

I took three rapid steps back, away from the table, but not before grabbing the bronze vessel. It had a thick, heavy base, and could serve as a crude weapon. As I moved away, some of the purple liquid splashed down onto the stone floor.

To my surprise, a girl's head rose into view as she climbed the spiral staircase – the face, beautiful and serene, the black hair braided with green stones, the neck long and graceful, then a narrow waist and very long legs. I suddenly noticed the silver tree-fern tattoo on her forehead.

She wore a black dress that was little more than a shift. It was as if someone had simply cut three functional holes for her arms and head, for there was no evidence of stitching. The dress was tied at the waist with a white sash, and very short, revealing a long expanse of thigh. Her feet were clad in silver shoes which seemed to be made of something metallic but flexed as she walked.

She halted at the top of the circular stairwell. Very slowly I moved round the table towards her. Then, to my amazement, she spoke to me in my own language.

'You're spilling the wine,' she said softly.

I was so astonished that I immediately spilled some more:

the words might have been spoken by a woman from Gindeen. The girl's manner was soft and welcoming, and her voice held no trace of rebuke or hostility.

I studied her face. It was soft and feminine, but with a fierce radiance blazing from the brown eyes. Her skin was brown too, far darker than that of the Genthai, contrasting with the pale-skinned, yellow-haired people I'd stayed with. Nor was there any hint of the unnatural green that tinged the flesh of the woman who rode the beast.

I carefully replaced the vessel on the table. No sooner had I done so than the girl came up and bent her head forward until her nose was close to my chest.

Suddenly, for the first time since her appearance, I was aware that I was naked. She touched my chest.

'You're sticky. You need to wash,' she said, wrinkling her nose. 'Don't you wash before you eat?'

I shrugged. 'I'd be happy to wash, but where's the water?'

She seized me by the wrist, her grip gentle but firm, and led me towards the recess in the wall where I'd urinated, pointing at the oblong depression in the stone floor.

Obediently I stepped in, and she pressed a small area of darker stone: instantly, water fell in a heavy shower from the ceiling. It was cold, and I shuddered and gasped. But then, wasting no time, I began to sluice the water under my arms.

The girl left me to it, and for a few moments I simply enjoyed the feel of the water on my skin.

At last I was done and, copying the girl, I placed my fingers to the dark stone and smiled as the water slowed and then trickled away to nothing. As I started to brush the water off myself, the girl reappeared holding out a green towel.

For a few moments she stood there watching me dry myself, but then disappeared again. I wrapped myself in the towel and headed back towards the table.

There were two stools there now, one on either side of the table, and the girl was holding out a black shift like the one she wore. I accepted it, let the towel fall to the ground and pulled it on over my head. She offered me a white sash, which I tied loosely about my waist, and then gestured towards the nearest of the wooden stools.

I nodded, smiled and sat down, whereupon the girl filled a crystal goblet from the bronze decanter and held it out to me. I waited until she'd filled her own before drinking thirstily. It was wine – and far superior to that produced by the vineyards north of Gindeen. I smiled and was about to tell her as much when she spoke.

'Why are you here in our land?' she asked. 'What is your purpose? My lady wishes to know.'

I smiled. 'I'm here to explore new lands and learn the wisdom of their peoples,' I lied. 'I'm a scholar who seeks knowledge and new cultures.'

'A scholar with a sword?' she asked, lifting the wine to her lips and taking a sip.

'A scholar must arm himself against the dangers he encounters. But tell your lady that I come in peace.'

The girl took another sip of wine. 'You fought like a warrior. Many of my lady's vassals died at your hands – you and your companion – but she will soon judge you. In the meantime we have work to do. I have been allowed seven days in which to teach you as much of our language as you can absorb.'

'Why do I need to learn it,' I asked, 'when you speak mine so beautifully?'

She frowned. 'It would not be proper for my lady to speak your tongue. It is you who are the stranger, and the law decrees that you must either speak our tongue or remain unheard. And if you cannot be heard, you are no better than a beast of the field, only fit for slaughter.'

The situation was clear. I had no choice. 'Then let the first lesson begin,' I invited her.

'Finish your glass of wine so that it may lubricate your memory,' she commanded.

I smiled, thinking that she was joking, but I drained my glass.

'Firstly I will teach you the names of things; then the names of actions; finally I will show you how to link these in such a way that others may understand you. In seven days, unless you prove stupid, you will meet with the minimum demands of the law. Either that or you will die.'

'What's the name of the creature your lady rides?' I asked. 'I've never seen anything like it. And are there no horses here? Do you know what a horse is?'

'My lady rides a rasire,' the girl replied. 'Only those of high rank are permitted such mounts. They are sometimes armoured and used in battle.'

I had heard the word *rasire* before. They were the squat humanoid figures who served the Trader. They had carried the heavy cylinder containing the shatek that Ada had bought to create Thrym, a sentient lac. This creature looked very different.

'A horse is called an *agnwan*,' the girl continued, 'but agnwana are only ridden by barbarians such as you. If you survive, you will soon see many agnwana. Perhaps you miss the mounts you and your seven companions rode when you entered our land from your homeland, which we call *Kisetorian Dutred*. Every stage of your journey has been observed.'

'Kisetorian Dutred?' I said aloud, trying out the words on my tongue. 'Do the words have a meaning?'

'No, the meaning has been lost, but there are other names for your homeland – a forbidden place that none may visit. Some refer to it as *Danur*, which means the Place of the Beast, for ancient legend tells of a ferocious beast imprisoned there behind the cloud, and warns that we must be careful lest it awake and devour the whole world. Of course, it is just a story, and we are strong and fear nothing that breathes.'

'What do you call this building?' I asked, gesturing towards the walls.

'This is a *krie-kore*, which is a way station or fortress that belongs to my lady. We will remain here until she has passed judgement on you.'

'Then I must prepare myself,' I said. 'Please teach me all the words I must know.'

I then did a very odd thing. There was something about this girl that pushed aside all my inhibitions.

'What do you call these?' I asked, reaching across the table and touching her lips with my forefinger.

Rather than flinch away or feign outrage, she smiled warmly. 'Lips are called *eileas*, and this is called an *itlea*,' she said, holding her tongue. 'We will begin with parts of the body and move outwards to explore the world. But first let us deal with our names. Your name is Leif. May I use your name when speaking to you?'

'Of course,' I answered.

'Then you may use my name also. I am called Peri.'

This was puzzling. How did she know my name? I wondered. Had I called it out in my sleep? And how did she speak my language so perfectly? However, I kept such questions to myself and concentrated on learning as many words as possible.

Peri spoke quickly, rarely repeating a word more than twice, but my memory was sharp, and no sooner had a word been spoken than it was fixed in my head. Whether it was anything to do with the wine, as she'd seemed to suggest, I couldn't say; if so, it had the opposite effect to any wine I'd drunk before.

The lesson seemed to last for hours, but my concentration didn't flag. At last, very suddenly, a great weariness came upon me and I felt my eyes closing and my head growing heavy.

'We have done enough for today,' Peri declared. 'Sleep now so that what you have learned will be fixed in your mind.'

I was only too glad to obey, so I went over to the recess and lay down upon the pallet. Within moments I was sound asleep.

The moment I awoke I was aware that something had changed. The air was cooler and the torchlight was weak, so that there were areas of shadow in the chamber.

I got to my feet and approached the table. The dishes were now empty, and the wine and the goblets had been removed, replaced by a small glass vessel containing a clear liquid. My mouth was dry, so I poured some into a glass and sipped it carefully.

It was fresh-tasting water, and I drank two glasses before my thirst was satisfied. It was then that I heard a faint noise from the pit by the far wall.

It sounded like something sharp scratching against stone.

Warily I went to investigate and, as I drew closer, I heard it again. When I'd peered into it the first night, I'd seen nothing but blackness. Now the dim torchlight would illuminate anything that lay below.

I knelt by the edge of the pit, peered down – and saw a face looking up at me. My heart missed a beat, and I almost recoiled in surprise, for the face was female.

It was Peri, the girl who had been teaching me her language.

I was about to call out her name, but then the face moved away into a dark tunnel beneath the floor.

With a sense of shock and horror, I now saw the legs and body upon which that head was mounted, and my stomach turned over.

The body glistened black, as if oiled, and there were multi-jointed legs – six at least – that mercifully carried the creature away out of sight.

The creature was more insect than human; more monster than animal. It was a shatek.

I crouched by the edge of the pit, desperately trying to regain my composure.

I'd assumed that I was dealing with humans; strange humans with a technology I'd never encountered before – I remembered the purple sparks emerging from the woman's finger that had caused me to fall unconscious.

I'd been wrong. This was a multiple entity, a creature similar to Hob, with many selves, given birth to by a shatek. The warriors with their strange armour of blue rings were also part of the entity. Its selves varied, but there was a high mind that peered through every one of its eyes. Ada had called that consciousness the *gorestad*.

When I talked to Peri, I was in communication with the total entity.

There was no doubt about it: I was the prisoner of a djinni.

THE MUSEUM OF LIGHTS

Human cities were once bathed in light that
obscured the stars.
That shall be so again.
But darkness always returns.

Amabramdata: the Genthai Book of Prophecy

KWIN

At the second party I was more careful and drank just one
small glass of punch.

I danced with Goodwin, and we talked a little, but judging
by the glances he gave me whenever he thought I wasn't
looking, he wasn't happy. He wasn't getting the same
responses from me: instead of giggling at his jokes I just
smiled politely.

The evening dragged on, but at last my father and I were
able to go home. I sighed with relief. Just one more party and
it would finally be over.

As my father had explained, the third one was to be on
neutral territory. Goodwin's family suggested a venue and
offered to pay for everything. They wanted to throw a really

big party. After much discussion, my father agreed. It was to be held in a function room in a wing of the Protector's palace.

That caught my attention. I was eager to visit the palace. The east wing was occupied by the Genthai and the west by the City Directorate; my father went there for meetings, but I never got to accompany him. There were all sorts of rumours about what was inside. One part was supposed to be a museum, with artefacts from Earth's distant past, dating from a time long before humans were defeated by the djinn.

My father told me that all the old wealthy families would be at the party. I suppose extravagance and huge guest lists matched the mood in the city. Confidence had returned. The retribution from beyond the Barrier hadn't happened and Hob remained in his citadel. People were starting to enjoy themselves again.

The function room proved to be disappointing. It was rather small and no different to the staid drawing rooms of the wealthier homes in the city.

I was wearing my third new dress. It was another long, lacy thing with the hem trailing on the floor and the sleeves getting in the way. It took all my will power to stop myself hitching them up.

Hidden underneath that dress I was wearing the red Trig boots Leif had bought me, and up my left sleeve was the blade I always carried around Gindeen.

It made me feel better; I smiled to myself when I thought how easily I could put paid to my betrothal simply by raising the hem of my dress and showing them who I really was.

But although I began the evening in a wintry mood, it

gradually thawed. After all, I was seeing Goodwin for the last time, so I decided to make the best of things. Perhaps my smile was warmer this time; perhaps, without realizing it, I was more encouraging; whatever the reason, he paused at the end of a dance, smiled warmly and made a suggestion.

'I'd like to show you more of the palace – something special. It's on the floor below this. My father has been given special permission for us to have access to it.'

'What is it?' I asked, my curiosity beginning to stir.

'Come with me and find out!' he challenged.

Intrigued, I followed him out of the function room and down a flight of steps to an oaken door. Goodwin produced a key, unlocked it and led the way into a vast room, lit by flickering torches showing large glass cases and sturdy chests of drawers.

'It's a museum of natural history!' I cried.

The glass cases were mostly filled with stuffed birds. There were no mammals, I realized as I studied the exhibits.

'Are the mammals kept elsewhere?' I asked.

Goodwin shook his head. 'This was an island of birds. There were dogs, cats and farm animals such as sheep and cattle, but hardly any wild mammals until the djinn introduced them.'

'We're on an island?'

'That's what my father believes. There's evidence here to suggest it. If the maps we've found are genuine, they confirm that. We seem to be on an island, and there's another one, roughly equal in size, just to the south.'

As well as being joint owner of a large gambling house, Goodwin's father was the head of Gindeen's Historical

Society – a group of passionate amateur historians who delved into the past, attempting to tease out its secrets.

'Hey, would you like to see something really ugly?' Goodwin asked. 'Even uglier than my mug?'

I smiled and gave the required response: 'You're not ugly,' I told him. 'Far from it.'

'Compared with this I'm not,' he said, walking across to a chest of drawers and opening the top one. I joined him there. The drawer had a glass top, and beneath it were rows of insects.

'Wrong drawer!' he said, and pushed it back into place before opening another one. 'Ah – this is the one. Just take a look at that!'

Once again there were rows of insects beneath the glass, but one immediately caught my eye because it was enormous.

'That's called a *weta*,' Goodwin told me. 'There are none alive within the Barrier, but maybe they still exist beyond it. It seems that they were quite rare; attempts were made to protect them – though why anyone would want to save such an ugly creature I can't imagine.'

I stared at it with a mixture of astonishment and revulsion. I imagined waking up in the dark to find that huge insect crawling across my face.

'Do you know what my father calls this museum?' Goodwin asked me.

I shrugged.

'He's named it the Museum of Lights.'

I looked up at the torches flickering with yellow light.

Goodwin saw the direction of my gaze and shook his head. 'Not the torches. These are special lights – they are down on a lower floor. Want to see?'

I followed him down another flight of steps to another oaken door. This time, when he pushed it open, I could see only darkness within.

'You first,' I said, suddenly suspicious. I didn't know what he had in mind, but I could guess. If I was right, Goodwin had made a big mistake.

But he simply reached through the door to something on the wall. I heard a click, and the room was suddenly, magically, filled with light. I followed him inside, gazing up in wonder at the source of the light – glass orbs attached to the ceiling. I could hear a noise too: a faint humming from somewhere beyond the nearest wall.

'What causes the light is called electricity!' Goodwin announced. 'Cities all over the world were once lit by this power. But this isn't the only reason why my father chose the name of the museum. Prepare to be amazed!'

I saw on the wall what looked like a large landscape picture frame, though it contained only a piece of silver-coloured glass. But then Goodwin touched a strip of dark material beneath it, and the frame filled with light. Suddenly there was an astonishing bird's-eye view of a conical mountain with smoke rising from its summit.

It was like looking through clear glass into the real world. There was depth, and a sense of being at a great height. I felt giddy and was afraid of falling. Then we plunged down at speed so that my heart was in my mouth. We were closer now, and I could see a stream of red fire flowing down the rocky grey mountainside. The mountain was hollow and filled with fire.

'It's a fire mountain, properly called a *volcano*,' Goodwin told me. 'Once the two islands were full of them, and there were things called earthquakes, where the ground shook so violently that whole cities collapsed into dust. But the djinn did something and that doesn't happen any more. There are records here of how they reshaped the landscape, flattening some mountains while raising others, and changing the routes of rivers.'

Now the scene within the frame faded back to the original silver. Goodwin came over and placed his hands on my shoulders. He was a head taller than me, and I looked up too slowly to realize what he was about to do.

A second later, his arms were around me and his lips were pressing hard against mine. It happened so quickly that I barely had time to react. But as I brought my left hand up to his chest, intending to push him away, the lights went out. We were plunged into absolute darkness.

I heard heavy footsteps, then felt Goodwin being tugged away from me, so violently that I almost overbalanced.

He screamed just once, his voice high and shrill, like a pig being slaughtered. It was cut off very suddenly with a loud cracking sound.

The silence that followed was terrifying. I became aware that something was standing close by in the darkness. I could hear heavy breathing that reminded me of lacs after fighting in the arena. Was it indeed a lac – one of the feral ones that lived in the labyrinth of tunnels below the Wheel?

I began to tremble with fear, but I took a slow, deep breath to calm myself and allowed the dagger to slip out of my sleeve into my left hand.

Then a deep voice spoke to me out of the darkness. 'Raise that blade against me and I will snap your neck like a twig.'

'Who are you?' I demanded, hearing the tremor in my voice as I spoke.

'I slew your sister's husband, Kern, and soon I will slay the one you love. But I will not snap Leif's neck as I did that of the foolish boy you just embraced. That is too easy a death. I will kill him slowly, and he will experience extreme torment.'

And then I realized that I was alone in the darkness with Hob.

THE ART OF WAR

A shalatan is a warrior djinn with great skill in
generating selves to perform particular tasks.

One such self is known as a peri. It functions as
an ambassador to other djinn and is proficient in
languages.

The History of the Conflict by Eitel the Pessimist

LEIF

Suddenly the torches flared up, so that the chamber was once
more filled with bright light. Despite this, the manner of its
arrival unnerved me, and I stared up at the torch directly
above my head, wondering by what occult means the illumination had been achieved. A similar thing had happened when
Hob visited Arena 13.

It was then that I heard footsteps ringing on the spiral
stairs; I turned to see Peri emerging with a tray bearing two
goblets already filled with the purple wine. I followed her
to the table, seated myself on a stool and accepted a goblet,
sipping at the wine carefully while trying to control my
trembling hands.

'You look ill at ease,' Peri said. 'Did you not sleep well?'

I gestured towards the pit by the wall. 'I saw someone down there,' I said; 'a woman with your face. I thought it was you. But when I looked more carefully, I saw that it was something monstrous, a creature more insect than woman, a creature that scuttled on many legs rather than walking upon two. It was a creature called a shatek. You are a djinni!'

For a moment anger moved like a storm cloud across Peri's face; her eyes flashed dangerously, then she frowned and looked down at her feet. But when she looked up again, she was smiling.

'I am indeed what you say. Those you fought upon the bridge were part of another djinni, which was our vassal but then rebelled. Things are very much more complex than you can know. You should not always be so quick to judge what you do not understand,' Peri told me. 'What you saw in the pit was the mother of all who dwell within this krie-kore. We are all servants of my lady, and the shatek you glimpsed is the mother of us all. I am a peri – one who is proficient in all languages and modes of communication.'

'The shatek is your mother?' I asked.

Peri nodded. 'She is, but there is no need to fear her. She dwells on the lower level and will remain there. Even if you were foolhardy enough to venture below, she would not cause you serious harm – at least, not unless my lady so commanded. But I will tell you something to sharpen your concentration for the lesson ahead. If my lady decrees that you are to die, then it will be in the arms of my mother.'

My blood ran cold at that thought. I remembered how Ada had fed the lac to a shatek; it had been devoured and reborn as Thrym. I clearly remembered its screams of agony. I couldn't imagine a worse way to die.

I realized that the shatek below must be more powerful than the one that had given birth to Thrym, which had died immediately afterwards.

My sense of foreboding returned.

I applied myself to my studies until, at last, the day of my judgement arrived.

It seemed far longer than seven days, the periods of waking and sleeping hard to estimate. After each long lesson I was exhausted and slept; there were twenty-seven of them, though Peri assured me that less than a week had passed.

Strangely, I was finding it difficult to conceive of Peri as one of the selves of a djinni. I'd grown accustomed to her; she was almost like a human companion. I felt the urge to communicate with her, or maybe it was to do with the glass of wine that preceded every lesson . . .

On the morning of my judgement I showered and dressed in the clean robe that had been laid out for me. Then I ate and drank with Peri while I waited for the guards to come for me.

'Thank you for teaching me your language,' I said.

She smiled. 'If you answer my lady's questions carefully, using the language skills you have acquired, that will be my reward. I hope you are given the gift of life, Leif. If you are, we may soon meet again. And now I will teach you one final word. The word is *Shalatan*, which means "my lady" and is also the name of the djinni of which I am a part. It is the term you must use to address her when answering her questions. Say it softly and respectfully.'

'Of course I will,' I replied.

'It has been good to interact with you, Leif. When djinni talks to djinni, wishing to avoid conflict, it is the peri that facilitates the communication. If it is successful, we say that a *handshake* has occurred and *protocol* has been agreed. We have achieved that. It is a pity that you must be judged.'

'We humans also use the term "handshake", and it is done like this,' I said, gripping her right hand with my own.

She gave me a wide smile and stroked her thumb gently across the back of my hand. Then she withdrew her hand and, without a backward glance, descended the spiral steps.

I was left to face the guards. They were as I remembered them – tall men dressed in dark blue ring-armour carrying silver spears with three barbs close to the point. They simply gestured towards the open door and followed close at my heels until I emerged into the circular chamber.

Here were another six guards, all identical in dress and feature. Of course, they were all selves of the djinni. They stood with their backs to the curved wall, facing a simple wooden chair with a high back. Upon it was seated the one who would judge me.

Shalatan wore a blue dress with a black belt, the two daggers with the rams' heads tucked in on either side. There were no torches, but the light, which seemed to emanate from the walls, was very bright. Once again I wondered at the woman's beauty and her proud features. If anything, her skin looked even greener than before.

A spear-point prodded me towards her until *alsha*, the word for 'halt', was hissed at my back.

The woman smiled disdainfully, then spoke very slowly, to

make it as easy as possible for me to understand. But there was also mockery in her voice. 'You say you are a scholar,' she said. 'We too have scholars but, in addition to their wider knowledge, they each have a specialism. Is that true of you also?'

I knew that my story had not been believed, but I smiled and bowed and, in a sudden flash of intuition, suddenly knew how to answer.

'My own specialism is the art of war, Shalatan,' I answered. 'I am skilled in the methods of my own people and, in my travels, seek further knowledge.'

'What does a barbarian know of the arts of war?' she asked, her voice suddenly sharp with anger.

'I have a little skill, Shalatan,' I answered, 'and I am prepared to prove it. Place a weapon in my hands and I will fight and attempt to defeat any of your warriors you choose.'

I had taken a great chance in speaking so boldly, but I wanted her to see that I too was a warrior. For a moment I thought I'd made a terrible mistake.

She pointed her finger at me. I tensed, expecting the sudden loss of consciousness I'd experienced by the riverbank. But then her face softened and she lowered her hand.

'You show courage. You may indeed be both a scholar and a warrior, but you are also something else. I have examined the chart you were drawing; the chart that marks the route into our land. You are a spy, and for that you will certainly die. But I have not preserved your life so far for nothing. I intend to let others question you.

'Our own scholars, far to the north, have specialist knowledge of Danur. I could take you there blindfolded and bound in chains. But there is another way; one that depends on you.

Even a barbarian may understand what honour is. So, I ask you – are you a creature of honour?'

I bowed. 'Yes, Shalatan.'

'Will you keep your word?'

Once again I bowed and answered, 'Yes.'

'Then, if I take you with me rather than having you slain here, do you promise not to escape, not to lift a hand against me or mine?'

'I promise, Shalatan,' I said. 'You have my word.'

She smiled then; a triumphant smile. 'Then I will take you north to be questioned.'

They gave me clothes and boots – those that had been taken from me by the river. Then, to my surprise, they gave me back my shield and short sword.

Outside there was another surprise waiting for me: a mare with the very same saddle and bridle as my own dead mount, Laras; they must have been taken from her bloody carcass and brought here.

Then, as I drew closer, my hands and then my legs began to tremble, and I thought I might fall. The mare was identical to Laras – even to the dappling on her hind quarters and the patch of white below her right eye. And she seemed to know me, giving a whinny of welcome at my approach.

I rode alongside my escort towards the northern wall of the krie-kore. There Shalatan waited on her rasire; this time the beast was armoured with ridged black plates that fitted one over the other like the scales of a serpent. Ranked before the djinni were between six and seven hundred foot soldiers, all dressed in blue ring-armour.

Now, in addition to the spears, each carried an oblong shield and wore a short sword at his belt. Some – probably about a seventh of the total force – were also armed with a longbow carried over the shoulder.

My mount was attached to the armour of the rasire by means of a blue metal chain, long enough for me to make a complete circuit of the beast. The twenty warriors who formed a close escort on either side made it clear that I should stay well back, with the chain at its full extent.

Behind us were thirteen large wagons, much like the ones used by the people of Gindeen. Although the majority carried supplies, three were windowless, their doors sealed. Rather than wood, the upper sections of these three were made of copper and brass, and covered in ornate carvings of snakes and insect-like creatures.

I was curious as to what lay inside them, but was given no chance to investigate as their escort was equally vigilant.

It was good to get out of the krie-kore, and I went over the details of the map I'd memorized, adding to it as we rode north.

I had to continue to learn all I could. One day soon I would escape and take that knowledge with me back to Midgard.

On the morning of the third day we reached the top of a high cliff. On our right, a river fell in an avalanche of steaming white water onto rocks far below, drowning out everything else in its thunderous descent.

For several hours we followed that cliff west until, by degrees, the slope became less sheer and the river had been left far behind. But I remembered that, on my father's map, this same river curved north and then west, passing on either side of the city before reaching the ocean.

We were soon able to continue northwards, descending through trees which were not marked on my father's map; I added these new features to the one I held in my mind's eye.

The weather was growing colder and there was a chilly breeze blowing from the north. I knew that winter would soon be upon us.

At last the trees thinned out, and we began descending a steep slope; suddenly we could see everything around us. Far below lay a rich cultivated valley, crisscrossed with roads and irrigation channels; waterways fed by the great sweep of the river, which was now visible in the far distance. But it was the High Wall and the city directly before it that drew my gaze.

The wall barred further progress north. It was a formidable barrier, high and broad, built of grey stone, with a road running along at its base; it stretched as far as the eye could see, emerging from far beyond the distant Purple Hills to the east and flowing towards the shimmering Western Ocean. The city was also walled, and yet surrounded on all sides by water, as my father had indicated. For the great river, which had flowed north, had somehow been diverted by the wall to sweep westwards.

It rushed directly at it, but then, at the last possible moment, where it encountered the high bank that served as foundation for road and wall, curved sharply away to the west and sped towards the ocean. In doing so, it followed the High Wall before suddenly dividing to pass on either side of the walled city to form a fast-moving, defensive moat.

Yet water played an even greater part in the skilful design of the city; for other, seemingly artificial, waterways breached the walls, flowing under bridges to connect the moat to thirteen lakes, arranged in a great peripheral circle. Small sailing boats could be seen moored there, while larger vessels were at anchor against the four banks of the divided river.

The city, built of red stone, gleamed warmly in the autumn sun and contrasted with the dour grey of the wall beyond it. At its heart, surrounded by the thirteen lakes, was a great circular building, three storeys high, with thirteen domes upon its flat roof and a tall watchtower rising from its centre. Gardens and lawns surrounded each group of buildings, and from each, a bridge extended over a lake, leading to the huge circular building at the city's heart.

It struck me that there were more trees than buildings, which was puzzling. With space at a premium, the trees and grass greatly limited the number of dwellings.

I noted the obstacles – the wide, deep river and the High Wall – that would face a Genthai army. Perhaps the river might be crossed by constructing rafts but, although warriors might eventually scale its heights, there would be no way of getting horses over the wall. It stretched from the ocean to the hills.

So where was the gate indicated on my father's map?

At last my eyes found it. Beyond the city, heading towards the ocean, there was a single bridge that spanned the river after its two branches re-joined. That was also missing from the map, so I noted its position carefully.

This bridge gave direct access to a huge bronze gate set in the High Wall. So, assuming that the bridge was still intact when the army arrived, it would be possible to bypass the city. The gate itself looked formidable, but at least it was a gate rather than solid stone; gates could be rammed or torn from their hinges.

It had been well worth coming all this way, even though I'd got here as a captive. I had established the existence of the High Wall and the gate, and knew that a Genthai army could get here, tear down that gate and advance northwards. But I would like to take a closer look at the gate . . .

Once I'd learned its secrets I would escape. If I ventured further north, I would have little chance of returning unaided. Of course, in escaping I would be breaking my word to Shalatan, but she was my enemy. She and others of her kind had slain billions of humans and confined the rest within the Barrier. Our survival was at stake.

I would have to set my 'honour' aside.

BARSK AND ORL

Barsk and orl were created one for the other; the
first has a higher mind and is dominant, yet is still
dependent upon the orl that carries it.

Such binary djinn born of a shatek lack the power
to be born again of her love. By this limitation were
they shaped as warriors, for those who can die but
once fight most fiercely to hold onto life.

The History of the Conflict by Eitel the Pessimist

LEIF

It was almost a week after we had taken up residence in the
city that I saw a mounted barsk.

There was something chilling about the sighting, as if I'd
glimpsed the agent of my death, and in a sudden moment of
intuition I realized that none of us were safe here – not even
Shalatan herself.

I had been feeling at ease during the preceding days. Shalatan had been given the most northwesterly of the thirteen
quadrants. All that area, including the gardens, the lake and
the buildings, had been placed at her disposal. In addition,

there was a vast subterranean area, to which I alone was denied access. It was a dark zone into which Shalatan and her warriors and the thirteen wagons had descended on arrival.

A wide, steep path paved with red stones led down into a circular hollow in the earth, but it was barred by a huge rusty metal gate. I'd been witness to the slow opening of the gate, but then an escort had led me away to my quarters; later I was told that even my mare had been taken down into the darkness there.

However, to my surprise, I was no longer guarded, and they had left me my round shield and short sword; my quarters were far more comfortable than in the krie-kore, consisting of a hollow cube of stones set in an extensive hedged garden close to the city wall. Later I learned it was called a *hansha*, which roughly translated into 'the strangers' house', built to accommodate visiting representatives of other djinn.

It had no windows, and only one small metal door, which could be closed properly only from inside by sliding it across on metal tracks. In addition, there were a number of heavy iron bolts to secure it.

The apparently small exterior belied the generous space within. Above ground was a single, austere room with simple wooden chairs and a round wooden table polished to such a sheen that the surface was like a mirror. On the walls hung small torches, each set in a conical copper holder embellished with coiled serpents and lizards, their eyes made of green and yellow gems.

At the room's centre was a spiral staircase; as soon as my guards had left, I wasted no time in making the descent.

There I found five large underground rooms, two furnished with curtains, tapestries and soft leather couches; the third was a bedroom, and the fourth provided washing and sanitary facilities. The fifth was almost identical to the underground cell which had served as my home within the krie-kore.

Again, there were the recesses in the walls, and a deep well in the floor where a staircase spiralled down further; beside this were two chairs and a table covered with a green cloth. It even had a similar pit running along the far wall.

I had not investigated either the well or the pit at the krie-kore, but now the time was approaching when I needed to escape and return home. They might lead to a way out and I resolved to explore them.

I sat down at the table and waited patiently. No more than a few minutes had elapsed before I heard familiar footsteps and Peri's smiling face rose into view carrying a tray laden with food and drink.

'I didn't see you on the journey,' I said as she transferred the items to the table. 'At first I thought you'd been left behind, but I wondered if you were hidden away in one of the wagons. Was it one of those with brass sides?'

Peri smiled but did not answer; instead she offered me a glass of wine, and I took a mouthful. It began to warm my belly immediately.

'Are we going to continue with the lessons now?' I asked.

'Well, there are lots of new words for you to learn – some of them very important for anyone who stays in this city. I shall also begin teaching you the High Tongue, which is used for formal communications. But I'm going to leave further lessons until tomorrow so you can rest after the journey. You'll be quite safe – as long as you don't venture beyond the boundaries of the garden.'

'Why should I want to do that,' I asked, 'when I've everything I need here? Surely I'm perfectly safe within these walls.'

'Each of the thirteen zones in the city is given to one such as my lady,' Peri told me, 'but there is intense rivalry between the zones; any weakness could result in expulsion or worse. Those who entered the city most recently are the most vulnerable. Our intention is to go north, but we must earn that right. Only those of the strongest of the thirteen zones may pass through the bronze gate at will. And, at this moment, we are probably the weakest. So stay within the confines of house and garden and do nothing that may make my lady's position more difficult.'

'I'd like to see the bronze gate. Would that be possible?' I asked.

'Certainly not,' Peri said, frowning. 'You are a stranger here. Once you stray beyond the garden my lady can no longer protect you.'

I was eager to see the gate and then make my escape, but I hid my disappointment, and we ate in silence. Soon Peri took her leave, once more bidding me rest and promising to tell me more in the morning.

But before retiring for the night I climbed back up to ground level and carried one of the chairs out into the garden. It was cold but, despite the chill, I sat there in the dark for almost an hour watching the stars wheel slowly across the sky. They were the same stars that were visible within the Barrier and I began to feel the pull of home.

I was missing Kwin.

The following morning the news brought by Peri couldn't have been worse.

She began by elaborating further on the dangers within the city. In order to pass northwards through the bronze gate, Shalatan would have to demonstrate her worthiness through the combat skills of her warriors. It seemed that the large building at the centre of the city contained a great arena and that, in ten days, the Games would begin – contests fought to the death between representatives of the thirteen djinn. To come last would mean immediate expulsion from the city; to come first would earn Shalatan the key to the bronze gate.

It seemed clear to me that this was where Midgard's Wheel, with its thirteen arenas, originated. But that wooden building was a poor imitation of the dome at the centre of this city of the djinn.

'Then, if we're unable to proceed northwards,' I asked, 'can I not be judged?'

'There are none here who have sufficient knowledge to question you. And if such questioning and judgement cannot take place, then my lady must take your life. That is the law.'

'It's good of her to go to such lengths to get me a hearing,' I said.

Peri smiled. 'She does it more for herself than for you. Here, south of the High Wall, dwell the weak. To the north, beyond it, dwell the strong; those who compete to leave this isolated island.'

'We are on an island?' I asked in surprise.

'Yes, this city lies on this little island created by the course of the river; but we are also on a larger island surrounded by an ocean, with another island to the south. There are larger masses of land beyond us – continents where the most powerful djinn dwell. That is what my lady desires – to be with the strong rather than the weak. You have given her a reason to renew her struggle for position.'

A sudden chill gripped me as I realized the implications of what Peri was saying.

'The djinn to the north are more formidable than those I have seen so far?' I asked. Ada had mentioned other types of djinn, and warned of the evolution by which means they had probably become even more powerful than in the days of Empire. I was now facing the reality of what that actually meant. We were just a few thousand humans, and the world beyond our island teemed with djinn.

'Oh, yes,' answered Peri. 'That is certainly so. They are called *asscka*, and their selves form great armies mounted upon rasires. They also employ *barska* and *orla*, which are binary djinn, to fight alongside them and also function as warrior ambassadors. A barsk rides an orl, which runs upon two legs, faster than agnwana. They are fearsome dual beasts, and are terrible to behold. They serve asscka to police the lesser djinn and bring an end to conflicts.'

'I'd like to see one of those mighty djinn, Peri,' I said.

'If you survive, one day your wish to see asscka will be granted. But soon you will see barska and orla. Three binary djinn are on their way here now to oversee the Games that will decide our future.'

'Will I be able to visit the arena and watch them?' I asked.

I expected a firm refusal, but to my surprise Peri said she was certain that Shalatan would wish me to be there.

After this she started on my lessons in the High Tongue, but I found it hard to concentrate.

After she'd left me I had much to ponder. The latest information didn't bode well for an invading Genthai army and I wondered what further bad news awaited me to the north.

My first sight of a barsk was chilling indeed, but it was the orl that filled me with the greatest alarm.

One day I was walking briskly along the edge of the lake, shivering in the chill air. That hedge that bordered it was low and did not obstruct my view. I was looking at the great red-stone arena at the centre of the city. The Games were scheduled to begin within days and I was curious about the contests.

Would they follow the rules of the Trigladius fought in Arena 13?

Suddenly I heard a strange metallic boom that lingered long upon the air. It came from the west, from the ocean. In my mind was an image of the bronze gate in the High Wall, and I realized that it had just slammed shut after admitting the barska and orla, who were due to arrive that day.

I continued walking; surely they wouldn't come anywhere near the lake – they would be accommodated in the arena building – and in any case, never once had I met anyone on my walks. Peri had told me that it was safe on this side of the hedge during daylight; but on no account was I to go through the gap and cross the central bridge over the lake which led towards the arena.

When I finally turned to make my way back, all was quiet and still. There was a light powdering of snow on the ground – the first of the winter – but the sky was clear and the setting sun was reflected in the calm waters of the lake. On approaching the city, I'd seen boats on some of the lakes, but this one was empty.

I was walking away from the bridge when I heard a light, rhythmical drumming far behind me, carrying clearly through the still, silent air. It sounded like hooves – though not horses' hooves.

I glanced round – and saw something crossing the bridge towards me. For a moment I stared, and then the blood in my veins began to freeze.

It was a rider on the back of something that looked no larger than a horse – though there was something very strange about its gait. When I saw that it had only two legs, I turned and headed away from the lake towards my hansha. I walked as fast as I dared without breaking into a run. My sword and shield had been left behind – why should I carry them on a lakeside walk? But now I felt desperately vulnerable.

I risked another backward look and saw that the creature and its rider had reached the end of the bridge. They'd halted there, and seemed to be staring in my direction.

I hurried on, almost breaking into a run. Another glance told me that the pair were following me. So far, I'd been retracing my footsteps in the snow; now I veered left towards the city wall, away from my dwelling.

I told myself that I was being foolish: the barsk and orl weren't following me at all – just making their way to the entrance to the underground area, to confer with Shalatan and discuss the imminent Games.

However, another glance confirmed beyond all doubt that I was their target. On my left was a small postern gate in the wall, one that I'd often surreptitiously examined – only to find it sealed tight. It was another five hundred paces from there to the hansha.

I realized I couldn't escape, so I stopped. There was no way I could outrun the beast and its rider. Besides, to flee gave licence to the djinn to mark me as prey; Peri had promised that I'd be safe so long as I didn't venture out into the garden after dark. As the sun was still above the horizon, I should have nothing to fear.

I turned to face my pursuers, trying to control my breathing, imagining how Garrett would have reacted to this situation. Garrett had been the bravest of warriors. I could hear his laughter now, and the wild words that were always more than mere bravado: *Only one, Leif? Hardly worth my trouble. I'll leave him to you!*

The barsk brought his orl to a halt about ten human paces short of me.

The barsk was terrifying to look upon, but the creature it rode was even more intimidating. It was natural to assume that the rider controlled the mount, but for a few seconds I wasn't sure. The orl regarded me with malice, its almond-shaped eyes glittering with intelligence.

I'd seen a similar intelligence in the eyes of the rasire, but nothing that compared to this. I noted that the creature was slightly larger than the mount of a Genthai warrior, but not quite as bulky as the heavy dray horses used in Gindeen. In some ways it was not unlike a bird: it had the same swift, staccato, purposeful movements. But its legs were muscular and covered in green scales like those of a swamp lizard, and its body was bulky, ending in a long tail that twisted behind it like a fifth limb.

Its arms were wiry, and its hands had four fingers and an opposable thumb. The fingers curled and straightened rhythmically, and the nails were sharp and pointed and shone like small silver daggers. Each broad foot had three toes that ended in claws and, protruding backwards from the heel, a sharp triangular spur of white bone.

Its neck was longer than a horse's; this was the only part protected by armour – overlapping plates that resembled those worn by the rasire.

The head was massive, like a block of granite, with very small ears that twitched and moved in all directions, as if attempting to listen to all points of the compass simultaneously. The scales that covered its face and shoulders were somewhat darker than on the rest of its body and were edged with black. Even more terrifying than the malevolent eyes were the teeth: double rows of razor-edged incisors angled backwards into a mouth that hung open, as if ready to bite.

I saw how fearsome such a creature might prove in close combat: the legs being used to kick and disembowel; the hands to rip and tear or wield weapons; and the mouth to bite and twist, tearing flesh or even crunching through bone. What chance would a horse have against such an entity?

I tore my gaze away from the orl and looked up at its rider.

The barsk was shaped like a human, but there was one difference: it had four arms. Two of them held onto arcs of what looked like black bone protruding from the armoured neck of the orl, while the others held weapons – one a long barbed spear that was attached to the orl by a coil of chain; the other an axe, the blade balanced by a murderous spike.

Instantly I recognized the combat advantage afforded by the extra limbs. The arms holding the protrusions of bone were very muscular, far thicker than the two that wielded weapons. Genthai were difficult to unseat, but I judged that only in death would a barsk ever fall from its mount.

The creature was clad in black armour formed from small, overlapping plates that rippled as it breathed, and upon its chest was the insignia of a triple barb, filigreed in silver. The hands were sheathed in gloves of soft brown leather, and the only visible area of skin was on the face. A conical helmet covered the head, with a thin nose guard that stretched down towards the elongated chin. The nose must also be thin, I thought, for it was obscured by the metal, and the close-set eyes regarded me with a mixture of disdain and loathing.

Then the barsk spoke. Its accent was different to Peri's and Shalatan's and its syntax was extremely formal. It was using what Peri had termed the High Tongue, but by now I was able to understand most of what was said to me.

The barsk seemed to know who I was. It made no attempt to question me, but neither did it show any sign of attacking. No doubt, for this barsk warrior, it was unusual to encounter a human barbarian within the walls of a city; and it would be aware that its enemy was protected.

'Your presence here deeply offends me,' said the barsk.

'From this moment I command you to stay hidden within your dwelling. Unless chained, you are no longer free to wander outside.'

I smiled and spoke to it in the High Tongue. 'But is this not a place given to my lady? And do you not know that permission has already been granted for me to wander freely between the hansha and the hedge?'

The barsk seemed to stiffen, and gave a low hiss. The orl hissed in unison, and seemed to growl deep in its throat, making the armoured plates on its neck vibrate. The creature had understood my words and they had angered it.

'It was I who gave her permission to dwell here,' hissed the barsk. 'And I can rescind or limit that permission. Know only this: if I find you here again, you will belong to me. Firstly, I will question you. Then I will slay you. Within this city, I am now the law. Wherever I am is the law. And my words are the law. Do you understand?'

I bowed low. 'Aye, *Chacckan*, I will do your will,' I said, giving him the title for *Lord*, which Peri had told me was used for those who held high rank north of the wall. At that, the barsk seemed to relax and, with a final glare that was no doubt intended to cow me, turned the orl and rode away.

The encounter had unnerved me, but all I could think about were the problems faced by a Genthai archer seeking to shoot an arrow into the eye of either the barsk or its mount. It seemed to me that both would prove very tricky targets.

SOMETHING TOUCHED MY NECK

A sycoda djinni such as Hob thrives on the need for revenge.

He has a capacity for infinite cruelty.

The Manual of Nym

KWIN

It was so dark I couldn't see Hob, but I could still hear his heavy breathing. He was standing very close. I smelled his sour breath, tainted with old blood. Even without vision I had a sense of his size. In my imagination, he loomed over me like a giant.

I had no doubt that he intended to kill me, but I wouldn't make it easy for him. Despite his warning not to raise my dagger against him, I tensed my muscles, preparing to do just that. Fear made my heart flutter, but I still believed in myself. I had a chance and I intended to take it. I was fast enough to cut him before he snapped my neck. I readied myself, judging the distance to his throat.

'Put aside your little blade. I do not intend to kill you now,' Hob said. 'I'll defer that pleasure until later.'

'You killed Goodwin!' I exclaimed.

'His death was merciful and quick,' he replied. 'I prefer to kill slowly, and will do so again in future.'

'But why – why did you kill him?'

'His will be the first of many such deaths. There was an attempt to destroy me. When that failed, there was a rebellion against djinn rule. The Protector has been removed from office and imprisoned. That cannot be tolerated. He must be restored to power and the Genthai must withdraw from this city.

'I have pondered upon what has been done and carefully calculated my response,' Hob continued, his booming voice making the air reverberate around me. 'Until those conditions are met, I will kill and kill again, targeting those associated with that rebellion. I have spared your life, but will not do so the next time we meet. I intend to slay you in front of Leif. I will kill you slowly, and your suffering will be great – I will delight in witnessing the anguish on your faces. Tell Tyron that. Tell him also that he is on the long list of those I intend to kill. My retribution will be never ending. Even some of the innocent will suffer and die – even those who played no part in the rebellion.'

There was a long silence, apart from Hob's heavy breathing. Then he spoke again.

'You remind me of your mother.' His voice was suddenly much softer. 'You have her looks and, more importantly, her strength of mind. Yours is the kind of human mind that I shall enjoy breaking.'

'What do you know of my mother?' I demanded angrily.

I realized that Hob could see in the dark. He could see my face clearly, and must also have looked upon my mother's face before she died.

Hob didn't reply.

But then something touched my neck. My first reaction was to flinch away, but I forced myself not to step back. I realized that Hob was now stroking my neck with his cold fingers, from my jaw to my collar bone.

It was abhorrent to me, but it was also good: his voice had given me some clues, but now I knew exactly where he was in the darkness. I could judge the distance to my target.

Everything he'd said had stoked up the anger within me. I was already balanced on the balls of my feet. I was ready. This was the moment.

I took a step forward and lunged towards his throat. I was very, very fast and my blade was surely on target. But it simply sliced through the empty air.

Suddenly the lights went on again, and I saw that Hob was no longer there.

Slipping the blade back up my sleeve, I looked down and saw poor Goodwin. I knelt down beside him, avoiding the dead eyes staring up at the ceiling. There wasn't a mark on him, not a spot of blood. But he wasn't breathing and his head was tilted at an impossible angle, his neck snapped.

He'd been nice – attentive, clever and witty, and on our first encounter he'd made me laugh. I could have blamed it on the punch, but that would just be an excuse. I'd flirted with him, and if I hadn't done that, his parents wouldn't have made the proposal that had sealed his fate.

Then he wouldn't have been here with me when Hob appeared.

Poor Goodwin would still be alive.

*

There was no easy way to break the news. Back in the function room, everyone was smiling and nodding politely, sipping their drinks and being sociable.

Avoiding eye contact and attempting to compose myself, I passed through the guests, heading straight for my father.

He could read my face like a book: one glance told him that something was terribly wrong. We went outside, and I gave him a brief summary of what had happened and the threats Hob had made. By then I was trembling from head to foot.

My father took over. He informed the militia guarding the west wing of the palace and sent word to Konnit, the leader of the Genthai. This took just a few minutes. Next he spoke privately to Goodwin's parents. I was grateful that he didn't ask me to be there. He did his very best to prevent panic.

People panicked anyway.

The screams and sobs of Goodwin's mother were the catalyst. Soon everyone knew that Hob had slain Goodwin in the lower levels of the palace. They couldn't get out of the building fast enough.

Back home, my father called me up to his study, where we could talk in private. He made me search my memory and go over what had happened; to repeat Hob's threats word for word, as far as I could remember them. It was exhausting, and I was still feeling upset after Goodwin's death.

'I'm sorry I had to put you through that,' my father said, patting my hand when it was over, 'but I have to know exactly what he said. Ada told me that Hob is a type of djinni called a *sycoda*; they have skills that make them good interrogators, though spying and torture are their main functions. They're vindictive, and enjoy inflicting pain. Their threats are precise, and they rarely deviate from them.'

He sighed and reached for the bottle of red wine. Then he seemed to think better of it, lowered his hand and shook his head.

'The Genthai won't withdraw from the city and the Protector will certainly not be restored to power, so Hob will embark on his murderous attacks. It's clear that everyone involved in the plot against him will be targeted – that probably includes their families. We can tighten our security and assign guards wherever feasible, but people will die; we can't guard everybody. This is what I've been afraid of. It's going to be bad.'

'Hob said that I had my mother's face,' I said, watching my father's expression. His face grew pale – though any reference to my mother always made him sad.

'He was playing with you, Kwin; trying to hurt you in any way he could. He's a torturer, and sometimes he uses words as his instruments.'

'Would he have seen my mother?' I asked.

'No doubt. He shifts his shape and walks amongst us unseen. He might have passed her in the market place or glimpsed her in the yard as he strolled past this house. But he is right. I love both my daughters equally but you have your mother's face – and her indomitable will and fiery spirit too. Sometimes I'm too quick to chastise you – but it is because you remind me so much of her: I hit out in anger because of my own pain.'

Tears flowed from his eyes and I went over and hugged him until he was calmer. When I left, he was already reaching to pour himself a glass of red wine.

*

It started badly. Hob began by attacking farms that lay at some distance from the city. Whole families were slaughtered – men, women and even young children. Nobody was spared.

A dozen such attacks took place the night after Goodwin's death. Hob was using many of his selves to carry out the murders. After a second night of random slaughter, this time in the city, emergency measures were put into place. Genthai warriors had previously patrolled only the city outskirts and the main roads between Gindeen and Mypocine. Now they were permitted in the city to supplement the militia.

They also encircled Hob's citadel – though that achieved nothing. The killings continued. Either Hob was using secret tunnels to access his lair or, being a shape-shifter, many of his selves already walked amongst us unrecognized.

My father told me that I was to be assigned an armed guard who would accompany me whenever I left the house. I didn't argue. The danger was very real, although I thought Hob would wait for Leif's return and try to kill me then.

My guard was waiting in the yard, a tall, muscular figure in Genthai chain mail that came down to his knees. He also wore a black hood and a short cape buttoned to his chin. That was to conceal his throat-slit – for it was Thrym, the sentient lac created by Ada. Together, he and Leif had defeated Hob in the arena.

He nodded to me, and then followed me towards the admin building. At the door of my father's office he gave a little bow. 'I will wait outside,' he said. 'Call me if you need me.'

'Firstly, come in, Thrym. I'd like to ask you a few questions, if I may.' I was curious about him. He'd escorted Leif to his first meeting as mediator between the Genthai and the Wheel Directorate.

At that meeting Thrym had thrown a spear, slaying Cyro, who lorded it over the Commonality, where many lacs were stored. Cyro had been cruel and tyrannical, forcing those lacs to fight each other in an arena surrounded by long blades. Many had died appalling deaths, cut to ribbons by those blades. What he'd done was illegal, but because money was to be made, the powers that be had turned a blind eye.

After executing Cyro, Thrym had disappeared. Some thought he'd gone to join the feral lacs that were thought to live below the Commonality.

We entered the office and I brewed a herbal tea and poured it into two cups. I handed one to Thrym, then we sat down facing each other.

'What have you been doing with yourself?' I asked, smiling at him.

'Waiting for Leif to return,' he answered. 'My hope is that Hob will issue another challenge and we can fight him together once more.'

'But while you're waiting, what do you do?' I persisted.

'Sometimes I carry out tasks for Konnit. Sometimes I meet Ada and Tyron. We talk of the future and things that might come to pass. We plan.'

'They say that you went down to the area below the Commonality. Is that true?'

'Yes, I have been in contact with the feral lacs,' Thrym told me. 'Now that Cyro is dead and conditions have improved, some have chosen to return to the upper levels and now train with their previous masters.'

'You say that they have "chosen" to do that . . . I thought you were the only sentient lac. Are the others also aware?'

'They are not fully sentient, as I am, but they have a dim awareness. I am able to communicate with them in a way humans cannot. I am concerned for their welfare. Just as Leif, with his dual heritage, could talk to both Genthai and city dwellers, so I can mediate between humans and lacs. They deserve better treatment. Once we have destroyed Hob, I intend to represent their interests.'

'Yes, they've been badly treated,' I agreed. 'But some artificers, such as my father, have looked after them well. When you intercede for the lacs, I'll support you. I wish we could destroy Hob now!'

'The time to do so lies not too far in the future. But fear him not. While I watch over you, he will not touch a hair on your head.'

Either because of Thrym's presence or because of his own threat to kill me in front of Leif, Hob made no move against me – though others paid a terrible price.

On the fourth night of the massacres, a single farm was attacked. The farmer, his wife and two of his sons were slain. One son was spared.

It was Deinon.

Hob knew that he was being trained by my father, and told him he would also die, but at a later date. How scared Deinon must have been to find himself face to face with Hob, his family murdered.

Neighbours agreed to take care of the animals and he was

brought back to our house. It was days before he managed to regain any sort of composure.

On the seventh night six more farms were attacked, and precisely thirteen houses broken into in the city, every occupant slaughtered. But that night the Genthai had their first success: one of Hob's selves was caught out in the open and cut to pieces.

Most people thought that this would only provoke Hob. Terror gripped Gindeen and the surrounding countryside.

Like everybody else I was afraid of Hob, but I was even more terrified that Leif would not return. We had expected him back long before now. With every day that passed my sense of foreboding increased.

Then, in Gindeen, things reached crisis point.

Hob had demanded that the Genthai withdraw from the city and that the Protector be restored to power.

At last the Genthai gave their reply.

They executed the Protector.

WE RULE THE STARS

When djinn confront each other, a handshake is the
preliminary routine exchange of information to
establish identities and purpose.

It is the first stage in protocol.

The History of the Conflict by Eitel the Pessimist

LEIF

I was not permitted to watch the Games.

Shalatan asked that I be allowed to attend if I was chained,
but the barska and orla forbade it. They were now the law in
the city, and she was subject to their will.

I was frustrated. During the afternoon I stood in the open
doorway of my hansha, not daring to venture into the garden
in case I was being observed. The huge circular arena was
roofed, but I could still hear what was happening within.

There were drumbeats, cries and chants. Every so often
these sounds were punctuated by cries and shrill screams, as
if a combatant was in mortal agony.

That night Peri visited me and gave me some very bad
news.

'The barska and orla have demanded that Shalatan deliver you into their hands within the week. They say that you are a spy and must be executed.'

'Will she do that?' I asked.

'She has protested and will delay as long as possible, but eventually she must accede to their demands. I am sorry, Leif. I had hoped that we would travel north together.'

I realized that I needed to escape soon. However, I had to conceal my plans from Peri. I changed the subject. I was curious about the day's events.

'How did Shalatan's warriors fare today in the arena?' I asked.

Peri smiled. 'Lots were drawn to determine the order of combat. My lady's do not fight until tomorrow.'

'What's the nature of the combat?' I asked. 'What are the rules?'

'Djinni fights djinni, and the victor moves up the rankings while the loser moves down. All manner of weapons are permitted – though of course my lady does not enter the arena herself.'

'How is victory achieved?' I asked. I had been wondering about this. In Arena 13 a contest was won by cutting the flesh of a human combatant. In this arena, did they fight on until all the selves of a djinni were slain?

'I am the target. If I am killed, my lady loses.'

I looked at Peri in astonishment. I couldn't bear the thought of her being hurt, let alone slain. She was the nearest thing to a friend I had.

'Why you?' I asked.

'Because I am Peri the Communicator. Battles in the arena

are the ultimate communication. It is the method by which rank is determined. It is right that I should be the target.'

I was concerned about Peri, but I knew that, with this new threat to my life, I had to leave as soon as possible. In reaching the High Wall I had achieved everything our mission had hoped for. If I could make my way back to Midgard safely, Garrett would not have died in vain. Although I no longer had my father's map, I knew now that it was accurate, and the details were clear in my mind; we could now follow the safest route, avoiding the Grey City. Once we reached the High Wall, we would control the gate and could hold this position against the north.

The biggest threat to us on such a journey would be the winged creatures. But at least we now knew of that danger, and could perhaps devise a defence against them.

Each day I waited anxiously for Shalatan to return. To my relief, the first two battles were won by her warriors, but on the third day the unthinkable happened. Peri was slain.

As the warriors brought her bloodied corpse into the garden, I ran over, cradling her head, looking into her unseeing eyes and weeping. The warriors just stared at me, unmoved.

Then Shalatan drew near, and before I could speak she pointed her finger at me. Once more, my heart fluttered in my chest and I fell into darkness.

From that moment on I was confined in a small cell, deep underground, with food brought to me only once a day. But at last, after almost a week, the warriors took me to a circular chamber, which was identical to the one in the krie-kore. There I faced Shalatan, who was seated on a high chair, dressed as I had first seen her, with the ornate daggers at her belt and the black torc with the rubies at her throat.

I knew that it was my place to answer, not to question, but I was angry and still filled with grief for Peri.

'Why have I been so badly treated?' I cried.

To my surprise, Shalatan did not reprimand me; there was something that might have been compassion in her eyes. 'The barska and orla seek your life and demand that I surrender you to them tomorrow before the sun is high. I cannot refuse. I have been too tolerant: I have failed to keep you as a prisoner should be kept. As I taught you our language, we grew too close. That is my fault, and that is why they demand your life. Now it is over. But do not think that I give you to them willingly. My intention was to take you north for judgement. Were the choice still mine to make, this is what I would do. I did not wish it to end this way.'

'And I did not want Peri to die,' I said sadly.

For the first time Shalatan smiled. 'You still have much to learn. Peri is not dead. While our mother lives, how can she die? She will be born again of the shatek, as are we all. Death is temporary. While our mother lives, we cannot die.'

'Then let me see her one last time,' I begged.

Shalatan shook her head. 'She cannot yet speak. But she will still speak when you are dust. We will remember you, scholar.'

Then they took me back to my cell and I waited in the dark to be handed over to the barska. My mind kept returning to what Shalatan had said:

While our mother lives, we cannot die.

That was something else that I had learned. It was obvious

now – something that Ada would already know – but the key to destroying Hob was to slay the shatek he used to give birth to his selves. This should be our primary target.

They came for me that night, and I emerged from the darkness expecting to see a barsk and an orl.

Instead, there was a woman waiting just beyond the open garden gate. She was staring at the city wall and, beyond that, the High Wall. She wore a long gown and her feet were bare. For a moment I thought it was Peri, but at my approach she turned and the starlight revealed that it was Shalatan herself. Her imperious gaze looked me up and down, but then her expression seemed to soften and she moved towards the city wall, beckoning me to follow.

I glanced back and saw that my escort had halted just within the hansha, so I strode after Shalatan, slowing down as I came closer, realizing that she might not consider it fitting for me to walk alongside her.

But then, to my utter astonishment, she suddenly stopped and seized my right hand, holding it tightly, her eyes fixing on mine. It was the first time I'd stood so close to her – usually she'd been mounted on a rasire or seated on a chair – and I realized that she was as tall as I was.

'Does this contact of our hands disturb you, scholar?' she asked. 'Our previous handshake did not bother you.'

Something in her expression changed again. Her face softened, the pale, green-tinged skin seemed to darken and, with a sudden shock, I found myself gazing into the soft brown eyes of Peri. It only lasted for a moment. The eyes and skin couldn't really have changed colour – no doubt my imagination had played a trick on me – but I'd glimpsed the resemblance between Peri and Shalatan, her mistress.

'Don't you know, scholar, that we are one?' she asked me.

Still holding my hand, she began to stroke the back of it with her thumb, slowly and tenderly, as Peri had once done.

'It was I who shook your hand, I who taught you the words of our language,' Shalatan said softly. 'I who drank wine with you and broke bread – and also, clad in blue armour, slew my enemies. I fight and die, and am reborn from the womb of my mother to fight and die again. Seven hundred and thirteen we are. No more and no less. Seven hundred and thirteen is my number. And each of them I am, for we are one. I am a warrior djinni. I am Shalatan.'

My mind in a whirl, I began to count. There were seven hundred warriors. Then an additional four in Shalatan's personal guard, and sometimes another six. Peri and Shalatan herself brought the total to seven hundred and twelve. Then I remembered the shatek I'd seen scuttling along in the pit below my cell.

She was the mother of all within her krie-kore. Those who dwelt there were one creature, a beast with one mind and many selves. Shalatan was like Hob, but on a much bigger scale.

The world beyond the Barrier was populated by djinn like Hob. Although hundreds fought in the arena here, there were really only thirteen, one in each zone: thirteen djinn, each with a host of selves.

I'd already been aware of this fact because of my knowledge of Hob and my conversations with Ada, but only now, after listening to Shalatan's explanation, did I realize what it *really* meant and see it through her eyes. When I talked to Peri, I'd been speaking to the gorestad, and all Shalatan's selves shared that 'high mind'. They were truly one, and all of them had been listening to me.

Shalatan turned back to the wall. 'We must hurry,' she whispered. 'There is little time remaining before the moon comes up.'

Still holding my hand, she led me across the grass towards the city wall. Soon we were following its gradual curve westwards. My heart leaped when I saw that we were heading towards the small postern gate that I'd noticed during my ramblings.

The gate was open and, to my astonishment, I saw that my mare, Laras, was waiting in the shadows beyond. My weapons were there too – the bow and arrows that I'd abandoned on the stone bridge. The two longswords, left near the Grey City, were in their scabbards on either side of the saddle, and my shield hung below the pommel. The others lay on the grass, gleaming faintly in the starlight.

'You brought my weapons?'

'Of course – we retrieved those you left behind.'

'But my horse – the agnwan – it was dead and now lives. How is it possible?'

Shalatan smiled. 'Many things can be reborn from the womb of a shatek,' she told me mysteriously.

My mind was filled with further questions, but I could see that she was growing impatient.

She suddenly released my hand. 'Take them,' she said. 'I return to a warrior what belongs to him.'

Astonished, I quickly lifted the short sword and thrust it

into the scabbard on my shoulder. Next I picked up the bow and the quiver, which was almost half full of arrows. I counted them quickly – there were twenty-two, as before. I slung the quiver over my shoulder, then attached the bow to the strap that hung from the horse's neck.

'Go quickly!' Shalatan commanded. 'Go directly towards the small bridge south. Tonight it is unguarded. Once across the river, ride for your life. Out on the plain, in the moonlight, you will be seen from the tower, and the barska and orla will follow. There are ten minutes before the moon rises, so use them well. This agnwan is swift and has stamina. If you get a good start and can keep ahead of your pursuers until dawn, they will probably give up the chase.'

I climbed onto Laras' back and looked down at Shalatan. 'Thank you for giving me this chance of life,' I said softly.

'Why do you think I've given you your freedom?' she asked me.

I smiled and shrugged. 'Out of generosity perhaps?'

'The barska and orla visited me again less than an hour ago. Now they tell me that *I* am to be sent north to be judged. They believe that I am contaminated because I have been close to you for so long. And I will no doubt be found guilty and sentenced to death; that would include all my selves, including my shatek. Our death would be final. That is their decision – I cannot change their will. Perhaps they are right: we have become too close and I have taught you too much. There is nothing more that they can do to me now. What more is there beyond judgement and death? So now I give you a chance of freedom.

'I do it not just for you, but for your people. After all, we djinn are the children of humans, and not all children hate their parents. I chose the human shape over others because it pleases me. Go back, scholar, and tell them what they face. Tell them how foolish they would be to invade our lands.'

'Invade?' I asked, about to protest my innocence.

Shalatan smiled. 'Do you think I am so easily fooled by a spy who carries a map – a map that was still being drawn? Go back now and make your report. Tell them there are djinn like me, each seven hundred and thirteen strong. Many Shalatans. And legions far greater than that. Numbers beyond counting. Tell them also of the barska and the orla. Then tell them that this is only the beginning: far greater terrors await them beyond the High Wall; you have only seen the least of the djinn warriors. Bid them stay safe in Danur, the land that has been allocated to them. Within its wall of mist, life is possible for your people. Were they to cross the Barrier, girded for war, they would be wiped off the face of this world for ever.' She pointed upwards to the sky. 'Djinn rule the stars,' she told me.

'You have reached the stars?' I asked in astonishment.

'Yes. Beyond this island there are vast continents ruled by djinn, but we have also reached worlds that orbit other suns like our own. We wish you to know that. Make the other humans see that. Make them see sense. That is why I have released you. If they invade, they cannot hope to win. I offer your people the chance of life. Go now in safety, and carry back the warning of one who is soon to die.'

'I will tell them what you have said, Shalatan,' I replied. 'And I thank you for this chance. And now, forgive me, but I must presume to advise you. Don't go meekly to your death.

Leave this city this very night and return to your krie-kore in the south. Gather your vassal djinn and fight those who pursue you. You are a warrior, and a warrior should die fighting. What better end is there?'

Shalatan smiled but did not reply.

I rode through the open gate, heading towards freedom, with the city wall on my left, the dark swathe of the river and the High Wall on my right.

After a few minutes I saw the small bridge on my left; as Shalatan had promised, it was unguarded, and I rode swiftly across while, beneath me, the waters surged westwards.

Once across, rather than heading south, retracing my route home, with the river on my right, I continued towards the ocean. The barska and orla might soon come in pursuit, but I needed to study that bronze gate and assess how easily it might be breached.

Laras whinnied at my change of direction, but I forced her on towards the gate.

Soon I was well beyond the red walls that marked the western boundary of the city; here the two rivers flowed together in a wide, deep channel, rushing towards the Western Ocean, no more than two leagues away. I could smell salt in the air and hear the distant crash and roar of waves. Now I came to the wide bridge spanning the river on my right, and set off across it, the mare's hooves thundering on the stones and echoing back from the High Wall.

The huge bronze gate was directly opposite the bridge; I saw now that it was circular, like a vast, dark mouth in the grey stone. It was fastened to the wall itself by great iron bolts, and was so large that it would have needed an army of men just to move it. But there were chains suspended from it, and two capstans south of the door, set in concrete plinths. It seemed likely that animals – probably rasire – were used for the task.

I glanced back and saw that the plain behind me was now bathed in moonlight. So high was the wall that the moon was still hidden behind it, but once I left it I'd be clearly visible to anyone on guard in the tall watchtower.

I studied the gate: it opened towards the river so that access was controlled by those on this side. That was strange, for the greater power lay beyond it to the north. Was it a defensive wall? I wondered.

Now, suddenly, I saw that it might have been built by others who had once ruled this land – perhaps even by the ancestors of my own people – to keep at bay some threat from the north. Whatever the truth of the matter, it might be used in that way again. It would take the Genthai army many weeks to reach this wall. However, once here, they could rest and gather their strength in safety, shielded by that High Wall.

I'd seen enough, so I turned round, sensing danger. Once I'd reached the south side of the bridge, I urged Laras into a gallop, emerging from the shadow of the High Wall as the moon rose up into the sky above it.

Then, from the watchtower, I heard the sudden harsh blare of a horn, echoing back and forth like mocking laughter.

I rode directly south, the sound of drumming hooves filling my mind, increasing my sense of urgency. Around me was flat farmland, with the occasional drainage ditch, which Laras jumped over easily, but in two or three miles the ground would begin to rise. Two miles after that, I'd be forced to dismount and lead her to the top of the steep incline.

I wondered how fast an orl carrying a barsk could run across this flat terrain. And could it climb the slopes ahead? An unworthy thought slipped into my mind: perhaps Shalatan had set me free on the orders of the barska and orla so that they could hunt me down for their pleasure.

I glanced back at the moon and saw, to my dismay, three distant riders. Even as I watched, they seemed to be gaining on me, and I cursed my foolishness in tarrying near the gate.

No. Shalatan had not betrayed me, I thought. I should have taken her advice. I should have ridden south at once. When I reached the hill, the pasture land would give way to scrub, then to trees, but I couldn't hope to throw my pursuers off my trail because there was only one direct route to the top. And I suddenly realized that they would probably catch me there.

Another backward glance established that they were already much nearer. I knew that there was now only one thing I could do; I heard Garrett's voice speaking inside my head:

There are only three. Hardly worth my trouble, Leif, so I'll leave them all to you. Kill them now, before you reach the slope!

LEIF THE WARRIOR

The moment Leif challenged the barska and orla is considered by most human historians to mark the beginning of the Djinn War.

The History of the Conflict by Eitel the Pessimist

LEIF

I brought my mare about in a tight curve, hardly checking her speed. Then, galloping directly towards the djinni on the left, I reached down for my bow. It was better to die here, facing my enemies, than to be cut down from behind.

I controlled Laras with my knees while I nocked an arrow. There were many unknown factors here. I couldn't be sure that Laras would continue on her present course long enough for me to get close enough. Djinn considered horses to be cowardly beasts. She might veer away in terror. Then again, the breeze was blowing from the west, from the ocean, and their scent might not reach her until they were very close.

Although a mounted Genthai archer could fire accurately at speed, he would never release an arrow without seeing a feasible target. The sky was cloudless and the moon was bright. Its silver light would give me a clear sight of my enemies. This was what Garrett had taught me; he had called it the 'economy of combat'. There would be no wasteful, wild releasing of arrows, so I was ready to put aside my bow and reach for another weapon if the situation dictated it.

Using the High Tongue, I called out loudly so that my enemies would hear my words clearly: 'I am the Beast from Danur come to devour you all! I come to take back my world!'

I was very close now: the orl was coming towards me with a curious rocking motion, its great head swaying from side to side, obscuring the moon at each stride, while on its back the barsk held in one arm a long barbed spear, angled up at forty-five degrees. Two further arms gripped the bone on the orl's neck, while the fourth was invisible.

The orl seemed to be holding no weapons, but its sharp nails glittered ominously in the moonlight. I could see the dangers I faced if I got near, and desperately sought some target for my arrows.

Then, as the orl's head swayed once more, I glimpsed an almond-shaped eye regarding me with hatred. I only saw it for a moment, but I took aim and released the arrow, already nocking a second to my bow as the first struck the target.

The arrow pierced its eye, and the orl's head twisted up in agony, enabling me to put another arrow alongside the first, so that their feathers were touching.

Now the orl was going down, buckling at the knees, and I took a third shot, this time at the eye of the barsk. This arrow missed and went skittering away, deflected by the nose guard, but we were very close now, and I sent the next flying into the barsk's left eye.

I nudged Laras with my knees, passing to the left of my foe. I wasn't skilled with the heavy longsword, but it had a good reach from horseback. I clipped the bow back into its strap and drew my longsword; gripping it two-handed, I swung it as we galloped by.

The orl was falling, head down, one hand groping for the ruin of its eye, while the barsk was probably already dead, held in position only by its two-handed grip. However, taking no chances, I struck the head of the barsk clean off its shoulders and brought my horse about, already returning the sword to its scabbard and reaching again for the bow. As I did so, Laras whinnied, as if in triumph.

I was now behind my pursuers, and I approached the second barsk from the side. The orl was beginning to come around towards me to avoid being attacked from the rear: I could see its neck armour – the green scales would surely deflect an arrow, even at close range. The barsk's black armour was also impenetrable, but now the orl lifted its tail – presumably to keep its balance when making such a tight turn.

Aiming by the silver light of the moon, I quickly sent an arrow into the soft tissue beneath the tail; the orl screamed and almost threw its rider, its neck twisting and jerking in agony. Once again, I swapped bow for longsword and, coming about in a tight arc, met barsk and orl head on, trying to unseat my black-mailed adversary. There was the clash of steel against steel, and sparks flew as my blade met the upright spear and slid down its length to strike the hand that gripped it.

Whether or not my blade pierced the mail, the barsk held onto its weapon. I felt a shudder run through my mare and looked down to see the orl raking its nails down her neck so that she reared up, almost unseating me.

But then, as Laras plunged down again, I swung the sword two-handed and cut off the orl's hands at the wrist. Blood gushed from the stumps and it screamed in agony once more.

I could see the third pair of barsk and orl closing in on us fast, so I disengaged and urged Laras southwards, reaching down to pat her. She didn't seem to be badly wounded, and although there was blood flowing down her neck, the orl's nails had perhaps not penetrated too deeply.

The third barsk was riding parallel to me, but gradually drawing closer; within minutes we would converge. However, the second one was falling behind – no doubt the orl was now losing a lot of blood.

The path was somewhere directly ahead; already there was scrub around me, and I could see the ground rising amongst the trees. To the south west, a dense thicket was visible and I nudged my horse towards this, desperate to find some cover.

This change of direction took the third barsk unawares and gained me a few precious seconds. I couldn't hope to lose it among the densely planted trees: I remembered the orl's sensitive, twitching ears. Even the faintest of sounds would lead it to me.

My plan was more desperate. The only real defence against creatures such as these was attack – a surprise attack – perhaps something they'd little experience of.

I reached the trees ahead of the third barsk and orl, hardly slowing, keeping my head low over Laras' neck. There were narrow avenues through the leafless saplings, becoming like tunnels where the branches met overhead – paths perhaps made by wild pigs.

I needed to keep moving – otherwise my enemies might be able to pinpoint my position or slow down as they approached the trees. I wanted them to follow me as quickly as possible.

I glanced right and left as my mare crashed through the thicket and, within moments, found just what I was looking for. I nudged her into a gap on the left and saw that luck was with me. Not only did the tree-tunnel take me in a new, unexpected direction; it brought me round in a tight arc to merge with a path that was almost parallel to the one I'd left. Now I was heading back in the opposite direction.

As I drew my short sword and hefted the round shield onto my left arm, I could hear the orl pounding along. I crashed out into the open just as it was about to enter the thicket, veered sharp left and, with the razor edge of my round shield, caught the barsk on the neck. I felt it sway backwards, but then I was past it, and charging directly at the second, wounded, pair.

A glance told me that this orl was close to death. It was limping, and dark blood was streaming from the stumps of its arms. But its rider, the barsk, was unhurt; it lifted an axe to meet my furious charge. As we clashed, I blocked the murderous spike and lunged horizontally towards the barsk's throat.

The exchange was not decisive, but the shock of the charge had brought the orl to its knees and the barsk was thrown clear, unable to cling onto the bone handles. As I brought my mare round, I saw that the barsk's helmet had been knocked off. It was on its knees, reaching for its axe.

I had very little time in which to act, so I sheathed my short sword and replaced my shield before lifting my bow. I loosed three arrows at the barsk in rapid succession. One found its neck, and it twitched and pitched forward onto the ground. But I was already charging towards the last pair, swapping weapons again, and holding my shield up to protect my head, my sword at forty-five degrees.

The third barsk had levelled its long spear at me, so I gripped the mare hard with my knees, ready to meet the shock of the impact. As we came together, I saw the silver triple barb on its chest armour and knew that I now faced the leader of the three, the creature I'd confronted in the garden.

I managed to deflect the deadly point of the spear, but the force of the impact threw me back off my mare. I hit the ground hard and rolled head over heels, coming to rest on my knees, still gripping my sword and shield.

I got swiftly to my feet and turned to face the deadly rider, the barsk, its spear once again levelled at me, and its mount, the orl, long sharp nails glittering like daggers as it charged towards me.

I planted my feet apart and prepared to meet the attack. I'd already decided to target the orl. Although once again I covered my head with my shield, this time I stepped to one side at the last moment so that the spear missed me completely.

Then, just as the orl's arms lunged towards me, I brought my shield's lower edge hard down onto them. The creature gave a long piercing scream as the shield sliced into its left arm, cutting right down to the bone. It pivoted round, its heavy tail snaking towards me.

I ducked, ending up flat on my face on the grass. I rolled away quickly as the barsk jabbed down at me with its spear, missing me by a hair's breadth.

Then I felt the breath of the orl on my face, foul with the stench of rotten meat, and again I used my shield, slicing into its open mouth, hearing the impact of metal on teeth; once again, the orl cried out and spun away, but this time I jumped to my feet and pursued it.

The barsk was struggling to control its mount; the moment it brought it to a halt I struck hard, driving the point of my sword through the orl's left eye, deep into its brain. Immediately it collapsed on its knees – though its rider still managed to hang on. In an instant I leaped up onto the back of the fallen orl and, with shield and sword, began to rain blows down onto the head, neck and shoulders of the barsk.

Dazed by the frenzied assault, it turned its head and looked up at me with bewildered eyes. Within seconds, its helmet had been knocked off; I brought my sword down hard, penetrating the skull and piercing the brain.

I slid off the back of the dead orl and knelt on the grass, trembling after my exertions. I took deep, slow breaths until the world stopped spinning about me.

Only now did I understand the scale of my achievement. Unaided, I'd slain three barska, along with their feared mounts. And there were many Genthai warriors like myself. Yes, in a year we might indeed reach the High Wall and defend it against any threat. Other deadly adversaries might lie beyond it, but this first stage was well within our capabilities. Barska, orla, rasires and creatures such as Shalatan might all fall under the onslaught of Genthai blades and arrows.

However, I now knew that stronger djinn lay on the other side of that wall, and there were more on the continents beyond this island.

I heard a noise, and turned to see my mare trotting towards me. I patted her, then checked the wounds to her neck. They were little more than scratches, and had already stopped bleeding. I was just about to mount and continue south when a sudden thought came to me.

Shalatan had spoken of being born again from the womb of her mother, and I'd heard tales about Hob that suggested he had the ability to regenerate his damaged selves.

What if the barska and orla could do the same? Within days, or even hours, they might continue their pursuit.

I decided to take no chances. They were binary djinn, so it was probably only necessary to deal with the barska. One could not fully function without the other.

I found the head of the first barsk, then used my sword to decapitate the other two bodies. That done, I rode south and, soon after dawn, reached the top of the incline and looked down upon the distant city and the High Wall.

It involved a big diversion to the east, but I had to be sure that the heads would be carried away beyond hope of recovery. At last I reached the high cliff where the water hurled itself onto the rocks below. Here, one by one, I cast the heads of the barska into the torrent and watched them disappear over the edge. They would be swept down past the walls of the city and on to the ocean, to provide food for whatever waited hungrily in its depths.

Then, with long weeks of travel ahead of me, I continued southwards. With me I brought a lot of useful information, along with the map, safe within my head.

GLAD TIDINGS

Although the Djinn War came as a surprise to the djinn, the Genthai had long anticipated it.

For the djinn, it was the worst of all wars – a civil war where protocol was abandoned and some performed handshakes with the Beast.

The History of the Conflict by Eitel the Pessimist

LEIF

The days passed quickly and I was making good progress. Finally I reached the stone bridge; it was almost noon and the air was clear and bright. My spirits were high, for my journey was progressing smoothly. Soon I'd be reunited with Kwin.

Then I saw that there were eight figures standing in the centre of the bridge. My good mood evaporated and I sensed danger. No doubt these were warriors from the fair-haired people that owed allegiance to Shalatan.

If so, they might attempt to kill me or make me their prisoner. After all, they wouldn't know that Shalatan had set me free. Or perhaps they were rebelling again. In any case, they would not take kindly to a human crossing their bridge.

I wondered whether to retreat and attempt to cross after dark, but I'd come so far and endured so much . . . I would not be stopped now. On impulse, I began to ride forward, but I didn't reach for my weapons.

I noted that the head of Garrett was no longer impaled upon a spike. No blood stains remained; no trace of the battle that we had fought there.

As I drew closer, to my surprise the men, dressed in skins, stepped aside, allowing me to pass, smiling and bowing. They were clearly from the same tribe who had looked after me for Shalatan. Three were warriors, but there were also two women and three children.

Looking more closely at them, I suspected that the women and children were the ones who'd been slain by Shalatan's blue-armoured warriors – the children thrown into the river, the women cut down with blades; now they lived again, having been reborn of a shatek. Life could be taken away so brutally and cruelly, but just as easily given back. This was the strange world of the djinn.

But it was not so for humans. If we fought the djinn, many of us would surely die, and our deaths would be final.

I was within sight of the Barrier when I had a surprise encounter.

I was camped close to the bank of the River Medie. It was a cold night; the ground was covered with frost and there was a thin covering of ice on the water. All was still, the stars bright overhead, and there wasn't a breath of air.

Suddenly I heard a sharp crack. Something burst up through the ice, its body gradually emerging from the water, and began to walk towards me. Ada had once told me about the many varied types of djinn. Although the ones I'd encountered on my travels, apart from the orla, had resembled humans, I knew that some were like insects or crustaceans in shape and could live underwater.

Fearing that I was about to be attacked, I reached for my short sword. But the entity walking towards me, water dripping from it, was human in shape.

With a shock, I saw that it was Peri. She was naked, and she paused at the edge of the river, her feet still in the ice-cold water – though she didn't shiver and looked perfectly at ease.

'It is good to see you, Leif,' she said with a smile.

I was happy to see her too. I'd gazed upon her dead body, but here she was, reborn.

'It's good to see you too, Peri. How did you do that?' I asked, pointing at the water and the path she'd taken through the shattered ice. It was then that I saw the change to her neck, just below the jaw. She had gills like a fish, although now she seemed to be breathing naturally.

'This was the only way I could catch you. It is important that we talk because I bring glad tidings from my lady.'

Had she taken my advice and fled south to defend her kriekore? 'Did you escape from the city?' I asked.

'There was no need,' Peri responded with a smile. 'Once you slew the barska and the orla, our rivals panicked. They couldn't comprehend that such a thing was possible. While their minds reeled with shock, we turned on them. Some we slew; others we drove away. It was glorious. The river was red with blood. Now we control the gate. We are your allies. Bring your army of humans and join with us at the High Wall.'

'But Shalatan bade me tell my people to remain inside the Barrier or face destruction!' I exclaimed.

'That was before we saw what you could do. That was before, together, we destroyed the barska and orla,' Peri told me.

'Together?' I asked.

Peri pointed to Laras. 'That agnwan is one of the seven hundred and thirteen. This also is Shalatan, made in the image of the creature you once rode. We carried you into battle. By your victory you have changed everything. Together we will ride north to death and glory. So give your people these glad tidings and urge them to join us. That is what my lady commands. But now we will perform the handshake and I will leave you.'

Peri came over and seized my right hand. Her flesh was ice-cold. She squeezed my hand and briefly stroked the back with her thumb. Then she smiled, mounted Laras and, without a backward glance, rode off into the distance.

I waited close to the Barrier for almost three days with little in the way of provisions. I knew that both Kwin and Tyron would be worried – I'd been away much longer than expected – almost four months. They might even think that I was dead.

I was unable to proceed because I didn't know how to contact the Medes. Perhaps Garrett had known, but he had taken that knowledge with him when he died.

In desperation, I hunted and killed a wolf, but it was so covered in parasites that I couldn't bring myself to eat it.

However, remembering Garrett's words and the *ghetta* he'd thrown into the river, I did keep a small piece of its fur.

At last a Mede became aware of my presence. He walked out of the boiling dark cloud and approached me, holding a blindfold.

'Is it as risky to return through the Barrier?' I asked, remembering the two warriors who had died. It would be terrible to have come so far and fall at the final hurdle.

'There is always risk,' the Mede replied.

'If I die, tell Konnit that Math's map is accurate – wait . . . I need paper and ink. There are things that I must record.'

Thus another half-day passed while the Mede brought me what I demanded. I drew the map from memory, adding the features we ourselves had encountered – marking a skull and crossbones near the Grey City to indicate the danger there. Then I wrote a brief account of what had happened and what I had learned. I gave it to the Mede to look after while I made the crossing.

Finally he blindfolded me and guided me back through the Barrier to Midgard. I heard voices and footsteps nearby, but at no point did I feel in any danger.

Then I was escorted by Genthai warriors back to Gindeen. After a week I was finally at the entrance to the city, but here I was met by one of Konnit's aides, who'd been ordered to take me to see him.

I wanted only to return to Tyron's house and see Kwin. 'I've been away for months,' I protested. 'I need to go home and show those concerned about me that I am safe and well. I also need to bathe and change my clothes.'

I could tell by the expression on the warrior's face that I was wasting my time.

'My orders are to bring you directly to our lord,' he said firmly. 'He is even now waiting to meet you. We must go.'

I sighed in frustration, but I knew that duty must come first. I was taken to the east wing of the palace. But when I entered the large chamber to make my report to Konnit, to my surprise there was one other person present – Ada.

Of course, she was the expert on the djinn; she would be able to evaluate what I'd learned. I began to give a detailed account of my journey: when I described the winged creatures that had slain our comrades and horses, Ada interrupted in order to tell us what she knew.

'Those flying creatures are called *gungara* – they form a component of many but not all high djinn: firstly there are the many selves of the djinn; secondly there is the gorestad, the high mind. The third component is the shatek, and the fourth the winged gungara, which devour and absorb the minds and flesh of enemies or other creatures whom the djinn choose to study. Using a shatek and the wurde, djinn can replicate and animate what the gungara have consumed.'

I was stunned by Ada's words. I remembered the silver fern-leaf tattoo on Shalatan's forehead, and the formation of the flock of gungara.

Of course, now it all made sense. The winged creatures must have been part of Shalatan, who had used the knowledge gained from my mare, Laras, to create a replica.

'I suppose we're fortunate that Hob doesn't have gungara,' I said.

'We are indeed, Leif,' Ada observed, 'but he is a sycoda. True sycoda have few selves – no more than thirteen – but Hob will have evolved. It would be good to know exactly how many selves he possesses; it will surely be many more than thirteen by now.'

I continued with my tale. When I came to Garrett's death, my voice trembled with emotion, my eyes filling with tears. Ada filled a cup of water from the jug on the table and passed it across to me. I sipped and tried to control my feelings.

'Garrett was a brave man and a great warrior,' said Konnit. 'He will never be forgotten. He died to give you a chance of life. You took that chance, and returned to us with information that might make victory possible.'

I nodded, but made no reply. I remembered Peri's words.

Together we will ride north to death and glory.

Did we really want that? Wasn't Shalatan's original advice more sensible?

I took a deep breath and went on. I told them of my experience as a prisoner and my conversations with Peri; of our journey to the city with the huge arena where djinni fought djinni for dominance and position.

'That is interesting,' Ada observed. 'At the height of the Human Empire we made djinni fight djinni in our arenas, and gambling was important, just as it is in Gindeen now. We used the djinn for our own entertainment, but they have continued with these forms of combat for reasons of their own.'

'This is how they work out their pecking order,' I said. 'The weaker djinn are those closer to the Barrier; the stronger ones lie further north. But we are on an island – there are larger masses of land with many more djinn. Shalatan also told me that some djinn have left this world and now rule the stars.'

'Is that possible?' Konnit asked in astonishment.

Ada smiled. 'I would have expected no less. We explored the inner planets of our solar system and had bases on the moon and on Mars. Djinn played an important part in that because, out there, they could function better than humans. I am not surprised to hear that they have reached worlds that orbit other suns.'

Next I told them about the gate, and then about my fight with the barska and orla. At first I did not go into details of the battle, but Konnit wanted a blow-by-blow account. He stared at me hard as I spoke.

'You fought exceptionally well,' he declared.

'It was either that or die,' I replied. 'The barska and orla do not expect to be challenged – that helped me. They rule through fear.'

'They do rule through fear, but there is more to it than that,' Ada said. 'They command respect because they are the agents of the asscka, the most powerful of all djinn. Each Shalatan has seven hundred and thirteen selves. An asscka can number many thousands. But you did well to defeat them, Leif. Such binary djinn are formidable warriors.'

Then I gave an account of my journey back to the Barrier, and my final meeting with Peri by the river.

'*Death and glory?* Is that *really* what she said?' asked Konnit.

'I would not lie, lord!' I protested.

'No, Leif, I do not question the veracity of your tale. It's just that I find her words astonishing. She offers us an alliance that is doomed to failure. She wishes us to join with her in an enterprise that will lead to our eventual destruction.'

'Her words are typical of warrior djinn such as Shalatan,' Ada said. 'They do not fear death, but only the manner of their dying. They wish to end in a blaze of glory. It is a tribute to you, Leif, that she changed her mind because of your success in defeating the barska and orla. From an enemy who used her gungara to slay any intruding humans, she changed into one who wishes to be our ally. No doubt she would use her vassal djinn as part of that alliance.'

'The vassal djinn had children. That's why I thought the ones on the bridge were human. Why would they have children when a self comes fully formed from a shatek?'

'Those children would never grow up,' Ada explained. 'The weaker djinn are closer to humans in the way they feel and think. They wish to replicate human family life and society. But beyond the High Wall you would find many strong asscka djinn, some barely recognizable as human. These are totally alien and think very differently to us. They might resemble insects or crustacea or assume hybrid forms.'

'What about the shateks?' I asked. 'Shalatan seemed to have only one, but it was the mother of *all* her selves. The one you used to create Thrym died after giving birth to just one.'

'That's because it was the lowest level of shatek. The highest djinn possess more than one shatek. An asscka might have a hundred and be capable of generating more. But let's take stock of what we have learned,' Ada said, nodding at me. 'Summarize it for us.'

'Firstly, we have learned what Ada probably already knew,' I said, looking at Konnit. 'That we can defeat Hob by destroying his shatek. We now also know that the djinn continually fight amongst themselves to determine their rank. That could also be used to our advantage. Shalatan offered us an alliance. Perhaps we could eventually ally ourselves with other djinn? Finally we have established that my father's map is accurate, and I have made a sketch,' I said, taking the map from my pocket and pushing it across the table to Konnit. 'We know the way to the High Wall.'

'I suspect that Hob will have more than one shatek by now,' Ada told me, then turned to face Konnit. 'What are your thoughts now?' she asked him.

He frowned, lifting his gaze from the map. 'There is much to digest, but it seems madness to ally ourselves with that single Shalatan. And as for finding others to augment such an alliance, is this possible? We might secure the area between here and the High Wall, but do we really wish to pit ourselves against the stronger djinn to the north?'

'It seems to me that djinn do not monitor Midgard,' Ada said. 'Consequently we are under no immediate threat. We should take Shalatan's original advice. We might have centuries in which to grow strong and develop our technology – I might be able to help get that started. We need a larger human population and there are ways to increase crop yields from the same amount of land. Time is on our side.'

'In the meantime we can take one important step to increase the security of both Genthai and city dwellers,' Konnit said. Then he paused and smiled at me. 'It's something close to your heart, Leif!'

'We can destroy Hob!' I exclaimed.

He nodded. 'Yes, it is time to finish him for good. During the past few weeks, despite our best efforts to contain him, he has slaughtered many people. He asked for the Protector to be reinstated and for the Genthai to withdraw from Gindeen. We gave him our answer by executing the Protector. We are now in a state of war. I fear that he will eventually use some terrible weapon against the city. We must kill him before he can do that! Tomorrow I will convene a full meeting of the Ruling Council and plan how this may be accomplished. But after talking to you and hearing your report, I have decided one thing already – we will use the gramagandar.'

I was shocked. That was the last thing I'd expected. This weapon destroyed the false flesh of which Hob and all djinn were formed. It was because humans had used this against the djinn that we had almost been destroyed and the survivors imprisoned within the Barrier. What would it be like to see Hob's selves killed by what was sometimes referred to as the 'Breath of the Wolf'?

'But, lord, I thought you intended to keep that as a surprise, if we ever moved against the djinn beyond the Barrier,' I said.

'From what you have told me, Leif, I think it will be a long time before we take an army across the Barrier – it probably won't happen in our lifetime. Besides, as Ada has suggested, we are not being watched here. The djinn won't know that we've deployed the gramagandar. We will only use one in case our enterprise fails. The others we will keep in reserve. But do not speak of that weapon or our plans to attack Hob to anyone but Tyron. He is the only one I trust with such knowledge. We know how gossip spreads – we don't want Hob to be forewarned. Now go and rest and gather your strength. No doubt you will be glad to see your friends again.'

That was very true – though it was Kwin I longed to see.

16

HOPE THEY NEVER FIND OUT

> The gramagandar is anathema to all djinn and its
> use is forbidden. It melts their flesh and sends them
> into the void.
>
> But both djinn and gramagandar are products of
> Nym, which offers them both life and death.
>
> *The Manual of Nym*

LEIF

As she was living and working at Tyron's house, I thought
Ada would come with me, but she stayed behind to discuss
things with Konnit, saying she'd be along later.

That was good because I wanted to see Kwin alone. I went
straight home, and she came running across the yard
towards me. My heart speeded up at the sight of her. How
had I managed to survive for so long without her?

She flung her arms around me and hugged me tightly.
'Leif! Leif! I was so afraid that something had happened to
you – that I'd never see you again. My father was worried
too. He expected you back last month for pre-season
training.'

'A lot has happened, Kwin, and I've much to tell you, but I'm all right,' I said, hugging her back.

'Father! Father!' she cried once she'd released me. 'Leif's back!'

Then she took my hand and led me into the house.

All I wanted was to be alone with her, but it was not to be. After a wash and a change of clothes, I was summoned into the dining room for a meal celebrating my return. Tyron, Ada, Deinon, Kwin, Teena and her small son Robbie were seated at the table.

I was hungry, but could barely take a mouthful of food because everybody was asking me questions, particularly Tyron. Deinon sat there quietly. Although he greeted me warmly, I noticed a sadness in his eyes.

I told them much of what had happened beyond the Barrier, but didn't go into every detail. Of course, Ada had heard my tale before.

'It's good to have you back, Leif,' Teena said as I brought my tale to an end. She seemed to have regained something of her sparkle. She was ruffling Robbie's fair hair as she spoke and he was smiling up at her.

A couple of nights a week she went with her child to the Respite House, where widows who'd lost husbands in Arena 13 gathered to comfort one another. Tyron had told me that she'd made a few friends there – he thought it was helping her.

'The news you bring is good,' Teena continued, 'and I think it gives us all hope for the future. We're not going to be attacked by the djinn after all. It's wonderful to have that shadow removed from our lives. You don't know how good that feels – to think that my son might grow up in safety.'

Nobody spoke for a while, but Tyron left his seat to pat her on the shoulder and Kwin kissed her on the cheek.

'Konnit tells me that Hob's been on the attack again,' I said. I'd done most of the talking so far; now I wanted to know what had happened in my absence. 'How bad has it been?'

There was a sudden silence.

Deinon got to his feet and, with his head bowed, left the room. Teena went after him.

'What's wrong?' I asked.

Tyron shook his head. 'The worst thing that could possibly have happened to poor Deinon. Hob has been preying on outlying farms, slaughtering whole families. To say that "Hob's been on the attack" is an understatement. He killed Deinon's father, mother and two brothers; however, he knew that Deinon was in my stable and let him live, threatening to kill him later.'

'Should I go and have a word with him?' I asked, starting to rise to my feet.

'It's best to leave it to Teena, Leif,' Tyron advised, easing me back down with a hand on my shoulder.

I wanted to offer Deinon some comfort, but I didn't know what to say. What did you say to someone who'd just lost his family? I remembered how I'd felt after Hob slew my mother and drove my father to suicide. Nothing anyone said could have made me feel better. I'd just wanted to be left alone.

Perhaps it would help if he knew that Hob would soon be dealt with once and for all. I'd have liked to announce our decision at the table, but I'd made a promise to Konnit, so I held my peace. This was something to tell Tyron in private.

'Deinon has been working very hard with Ada – that's helped him. His patterning keeps the pain at bay. You didn't tell us about Deinon, Leif,' Tyron said, frowning at me. 'He's a genius!'

Ada, who'd been training him in the arts of Nym – the patterning language that was used to communicate with the lacs fighting in Arena 13 – considered him to be a prodigy, but we'd kept this from Tyron. While I was away, the secret had finally got out.

'Here's a toast to Deinon,' Tyron said, lifting his glass of wine. 'I won't live for ever, and it's good to know that there'll be somebody to take my place. I always hoped to train a gifted patterner, just as Gunter trained me.'

Gunter was a legendary figure in Arena 13 combat. He'd also trained my father, Math, and patterned the lac that he'd used to defeat Hob in the arena. While I'd beaten Hob there just once, my father had managed it fifteen times.

We clinked glasses.

'And here's another toast,' Tyron continued. 'To my younger daughter, Kwin, who hopes to move up the Arena 13 rankings as soon as the new season begins! She's certainly good enough!'

This was excellent news and I smiled across at Kwin. I was pleased for her, but I was also worried. I would always be nervous when she was fighting.

Before I could be alone with Kwin, I had to talk to Tyron. He led the way to his study at the top of the house.

I sat across the desk, facing him. He sipped his glass of red wine while I told him about Konnit's plans.

'He intends to use that weapon – the gramagandar? Is that wise?' Tyron asked.

'It'll give us a greater chance of success. We need to kill all Hob's selves before he can use any powerful weapons of his own,' I replied.

Tyron frowned. 'In that case, I hope the djinn beyond the Barrier really aren't watching us. Ada once said that there were two insurrections by the djinn. In that first big battle, humans were successful because they used the gramagandar to destroy their djinn enemies. But there was a second insurrection, and this time the djinn won. They killed billions of humans, permitting just a few thousand to remain within the Barrier. Do you know why they committed such an atrocity?'

I nodded. 'It was because of the weapon that destroys false flesh. They fear the gramagandar and couldn't forgive us for using it.'

'Aye,' said Tyron grimly. 'Then let's hope they never find out that we used it against Hob. That might mean the end for us all.'

At last I was able to go to Kwin's room – though it wasn't quite the happy reunion I'd expected. Her feelings about my prolonged absence came pouring out.

'I was afraid, Leif. Terrified that I'd never see you again. I expected you back at least a month ago. I really did begin to fear the worst,' she said, hugging me again.

'It was the same for me. I missed you, Kwin,' I told her, looking into her eyes. 'There were times when I thought I'd never be able to come home. Ten of us crossed the Barrier, and I was the only one who came back.'

'Then next time Konnit asks you to go on a mission, I want

you to say no. Do you promise?' she asked, holding me at arm's length and staring back into my eyes.

I shook my head. 'I can't, Kwin. If we ever want to be free and safe, we have to take risks. There's Hob to be dealt with.'

'I was there when Hob killed for the first time this winter,' Kwin said.

'Who did he kill?' I asked.

'A boy called Goodwin.'

'Where did it happen?'

'There's a museum in the west wing of the palace – it happened there,' Kwin told me.

'Who else witnessed it?'

'Just me. We were alone together at the time,' she said, no longer meeting my gaze.

My heart gave a sickening lurch. Why had they been together? I wondered.

'After he killed Goodwin I thought he was going to kill me as well,' Kwin continued, 'but he knew who I was. He talked about you too. He made threats.'

I was horrified when she told me what had occurred. Hob had once promised to kill me only when I loved someone, saying he would kill that person first to increase my torment. Now it was clear that he really did intend to carry out his plan.

The moment I returned to the city, the danger to Kwin had intensified. I was very scared for her.

Kwin told me about Goodwin; although the boy was now dead, and Kwin had simply been trying to please her father, I couldn't help feeling a little jealous.

'I'm sorry – so sorry, Leif,' she told me, 'but I flirted with him. If I hadn't encouraged him, he wouldn't have been with me when Hob arrived. I'm responsible for his death, and I betrayed you too. If you want to finish with me, I'll understand . . .'

I put my hands on her shoulders and looked into her eyes. 'Did you want to be with him?' I asked. 'Would you rather have been with him than with me?' I felt terrible asking her such questions, but I couldn't help myself.

'No, Leif. Not even for one minute did I think that. We danced together and I laughed at his jokes. I enjoyed his company. That's the truth,' Kwin told me, meeting my gaze steadily.

I pulled her into a tight hug and then we kissed. When we drew apart again, I reached into my pocket and pulled out the small piece of wolf hide I'd stitched into the shape of a triangle. Then I held it out towards her.

'It's called a *ghetta*,' I told her with a smile. 'It's a love token. A Genthai warrior offers this to the woman he chooses to be his wife. In accepting it, she accepts him, and then gives it to her father, who then keeps it as proof of the warrior's commitment. I'm offering it to you now, Kwin.'

She took it and then put her arms around me.

'I accept,' she said softly into my shoulder, 'but you've got to promise that you'll never cross the Barrier again.'

I wanted to be able to say yes. I wanted to reassure her and make her happy. But I couldn't do it.

I shook my head and frowned. 'I can't make that promise, Kwin. I'd like to, but I can't. But I will say one thing – I think it extremely unlikely that any humans will cross the Barrier again. At least, not in our lifetime.'

She stared at me for a long time before she spoke again. 'I'll just say one more thing and then I'll let it drop. If you ever have to cross the Barrier again, I'm coming with you.'

As I made my way to the palace for the final meeting to plan the attack on Hob, I felt both nervous and excited. The revenge I had desired for so long was within touching distance. I wanted to see Hob destroyed for ever. But there was danger: he was powerful and resilient. Even if we used the gramagandar, there was no certainty of success.

We were seated around the large table where I had met Konnit after we'd defeated the Protector's Guard. The Genthai had transformed the east wing of the palace: there were tapestries on the walls depicting mounted warriors riding along a valley, the sky dominated by an immense horned moon. They called this the Wolf Moon, and it was the symbol of Thangandar, the wolf deity, who some believed would lead them to victory against the djinn beyond the Barrier.

Only in this meeting room were there chairs and a table – a concession to city dwellers; elsewhere the Genthai preferred to sit on the floor.

The meeting was amicable right until the end.

'We will keep our party small. Surprise and speed are more important than numbers, as we will have the gramagandar,' Konnit declared. 'I feel confident that we can put an end to Hob.'

He looked at each person in turn and then awaited a reply. Apart from me there were three others: Tyron, Ada and Wode.

Wode was Tyron's friend and also his rival. He was an

artificer and ran his own stable of Arena 13 combatants. He was a tall man who walked with a limp following an injury received fighting in the arena. In his day, he'd been a very successful combatant.

Tyron nodded at Konnit. 'Thrym wants to be a part of it: he's agreed to bring with him four feral lacs to carry and discharge the weapon.'

'That will be a more than useful addition to our party. The weapon is heavy, so it will free up four more of our warriors,' he said.

'How many warriors are we going to take?' I asked.

'No more than twenty in all,' Konnit replied. 'I'll pick the best – at least five archers. I will include Donat, who is the best with the short bow.'

'Garrett would have loved to be part of this,' I said, frowning.

'Yes, he will be missed,' Konnit agreed, his voice low. 'However, there is a warrior called Kalasar who will lead the swordsmen. He is big and can also fight with two longswords. Few apart from Garrett could do that.'

'One of the artificers wants to come with us. His name is Brid – he played an important part in our previous attempt on Hob's life,' Tyron told Konnit.

'He is welcome,' he replied.

'And what about you, Wode? Do you intend to be part of the attack?' Tyron said, turning to address him.

Wode shook his head. 'With my bad leg, I think I'd only be in the way. You'll need to move quickly through those tunnels. I'll organize a force to guard the Wheel. Not all Hob's selves will necessarily be in the citadel. Once your attack is under way, others might seek to do damage in the city.'

'That's true,' Tyron said. 'So be it.'

'It may not be necessary to kill all Hob's selves,' Ada pointed out. 'I could do what I attempted in the Wheel before the Protector's Guard intervened. With one of Hob's selves in our custody, I could put an end to all the others without penetrating too far into his citadel. That would also include the shateks he uses to create new selves.'

Konnit shook his head firmly. 'That I cannot permit. It is—'

'Don't you think I can do it?' Ada interrupted angrily. 'When the Protector's Guard entered the Green Room, I was just moments from destroying Hob!'

'I'm sure you could, but we cannot permit it, Ada,' Konnit declared, frowning as he looked across at Tyron, who nodded his head in agreement. 'We don't mean to question your abilities, and I am truly sorry if we have offended you in any way, but you are much too valuable to be put at risk in Hob's lair. You have an unparalleled knowledge of technology and, though there seems to be no immediate threat from beyond the Barrier, that could change, and then we would need you more than ever.'

Ada sighed and bowed her head. When she looked up, there were tears glistening in her eyes. 'You are right, Konnit. But I cannot forget what Hob did to Tal in the arena. I want to pay him back for that!'

Tal was Ada's husband, and I remembered his death with horror. He had fallen to his knees, and Hob had struck his head from his body. No wonder she wanted revenge. For a long time I too had been seeking revenge. I was glad that I'd be among those who set off to attack Hob's lair.

THE SYCODA SHATEK

Nym is immortal. Wurdes can never die.
Thus creatures formed from it shall inherit
eternal life.

The Manual of Nym

LEIF

Just before the sun dipped below the horizon, a bank of heavy
cloud began to build in the east and a breeze sprang up,
carrying with it a premonition of rain.

Then, with the dark, that rain came down, buffeting the
wooden dwellings and rattling their doors; a torrential rain
that turned the streets to mud, cleansing the market pave-
ments and driving the vultures to shelter beneath the
abandoned wagons by the canal terminus, where they hud-
dled, bedraggled and peevish.

Tyron was already driving the lead team of oxen into the
teeth of the storm, encouraging them up the hill that led ever
more steeply towards Hob's citadel.

We were taking the direct route, which Tyron and I had
used the night we went to buy back Kern's soul. In all, there

were four wagons, betraying not a glimmer of light in the driving rain.

Following close behind, led by Konnit, were mounted Genthai warriors wrapped in dark hooded cloaks.

My stomach had twisted into a knot, and the movement of the wagon was making me feel nauseous. We had been making preparations for two days, and that had given me too much time to think.

I felt sure that Hob would have anticipated our attack; that he might even have been warned; that he would be ready for us.

We believed that, for combat in the arena, Hob had reined himself in; his speed, his strength and his weaponry had conformed to the norms there. He had been prepared to operate within those parameters, perhaps to test himself in some way. But now there would be no restrictions . . .

As suddenly as it had begun, the rain ceased, and the clouds, already ripped apart, were blown away like fragments of rag across the horizon.

The moon shone down upon the land of Midgard then; a horned moon, thin and terrible, with the sharp promise of the Wolf. For it was the gramagandar, the Breath of the Wolf, that would give us a real hope of victory against the myriad selves of the rogue djinni.

Soon the great curved wall of Hob's citadel lay ahead, reflecting that moonlight: huge blocks of stone within a sheen of bronze that glittered with particles of crystal. As we passed by, I glanced into each of the small dark openings at its base that angled down underneath the citadel. They were used by Hob's servants – a degenerate type of tassel, more beast than human.

At last we stood right in front of the gate. Two of the Genthai would stay to guard the wagons. The outcome of our endeavour could not be predicted and our means of escape had to be protected.

As I leaped down off my wagon, I felt the damp chill of the night air; a fine spray fell from the towers, the legacy of the recent rain.

I looked upwards. This time Hob's citadel was not obscured by mist and I could see the thirteen spires clearly in the moonlight. They were of equal height, but each spire was different – twisted and corrugated with great craftsmanship, as if five artists, each at the peak of their abilities, had been in competition. And amidst them, invisible from the city below, were other structures, also of stone, yet as fine as the antennae of insects. They were similar to the structures on the roof of the krie-kore, the underground fortress where I had first been imprisoned by Shalatan.

The main structure from which the towers sprouted was embellished with grotesque ornaments: limbs and twisting necks supporting distorted, bestial faces that leered and sneered at those below. There were curves and ridges and dark recesses within which, I fancied, foul abominations might lurk, as if within a cave on a cliff face. Below these were windows, tall, sharp and angular, through which light seemed to flicker fitfully, as if its source continually waxed and waned.

I wondered how it was that such detail was visible in the moonlight, but then I realized that, in addition to the flickering light in the windows, the citadel was glowing from within; a glow that glittered and shimmered as the drops cascaded down.

There were cavernous openings, high-arched and daunting, all but one sealed by gates of bronze. Tyron had visited Hob's lair more than once and had told us that this small gate was always open – although for what purpose he didn't know. It was flung back to reveal only forbidding darkness, with just the faintest flicker of light beyond; and I saw that the dim light was a reflection from the wet flags of a courtyard.

My anxiety returned. I thought again of Hob, who'd lived in Midgard for so long he must surely have considered the possibility that an attack might one day be made upon his lair. He would therefore have a contingency plan; some countermeasure that Tyron and Konnit had not foreseen . . .

I remembered Peri saying that the djinn name for Midgard, the land within the Barrier, was Danur – the Place of the Beast. I had shouted at the barska and orla, telling them that I was the 'Beast from Danur'. I had assumed that the djinn thought humans were that beast, perhaps because they had constructed and used the gramagandar.

But what if it was Hob who was the beast: a being so dangerous and formidable that the djinn had also imprisoned him? If so, his power might be such that we could not hope to win.

And what forms might be taken by his other selves? They would not all necessarily look human.

There was just a few minutes' delay while we took up our positions. Tyron knew the layout of this section of Hob's lair; the intention was that five of us should go in through the courtyard and, without aid of torches, throw open one of the wide double doors to allow entry to the remainder of our force. The courtyard entrance was very narrow and, trapped within that bottleneck, we'd be unable to bring our full military strength to bear.

Without further delay, we passed through the portal and across the courtyard. Tyron was in the lead, I was directly behind him, with three Genthai warriors forming a tight knot to our rear — three archers armed with the short bow, which was deadly at medium range.

We crossed the courtyard and headed into a tunnel in single file. I felt a sense of claustrophobia and was glad to emerge into a vast hall with colonnades to either side and a sense of dark space above — a space that, no doubt, hid the base of at least one of the spires.

It was just as I remembered it from my last visit with Tyron. The two colonnades reflected each other, and beyond those pillars, on either side, were disturbing areas of darkness. At the far end of the hall were the three steps leading up to the throne, which was mercifully unoccupied.

Tyron and I had found Hob here, sitting on that throne. Tyron had bought back the head of Kern and, appalled and angered at the sight of his living head being kept in a box, I had drawn my blades. Tyron had guided them back into their sheaths, and then knelt before Hob, banging his head on the floor as he pleaded for my life.

There were no rustlings or whisperings this time; no sense of being watched. Just the echoes of our boots as we stepped cautiously onto the tiled marble floor.

Tyron betrayed no fear as he led the way forward, following the outer wall in a clockwise direction. He walked purposefully, with the confidence of a man who knew exactly where he was going and what he intended to do.

He had argued that Hob would never expect anyone to just walk boldly into his lair and throw open the main door. The audacity of the move should take the djinni by surprise. So far Tyron had been proved right. Already we'd reached the huge bronze door, but then, as Tyron reached up to draw back the first long heavy bolt, the hall suddenly began to grow darker, and instinctively I looked back at the throne and, even in the fading light, saw that it was now occupied. The dark-clad figure seated there looked like Hob as he'd appeared on my first visit.

It *was* Hob.

I looked back at the large hairless head with its hooked nose, which resembled the beak of a predatory eagle. The whites of his eyes were very large, the iris small and dark. I avoided his gaze. When I'd fought him in the arena he'd turned a fearsome glare upon me so that my legs had felt weak and I became temporarily in thrall to him.

I felt a spike of fear rise through my chest and into my throat. Tyron must have felt the same, for his hands had frozen on the heavy bolt; he was simply gazing back at the throne. But then, with a groan compounded of fear and frustration, he turned back to the door and drew back the first bolt with a great clang of steel upon bronze.

In response, Hob hissed like a reptile and came to his feet. He descended the three steps from the throne, and slowly began to approach the door, his eyes glowing brighter with each step. Tyron struggled with the second bolt like a man drowning, groaning as if in torment.

I turned towards the three Genthai, thinking to put their marksmanship to use. 'Fire!' I cried, pointing towards Hob.

But their hands were rigid upon their bows and their eyes were wide with terror. And suddenly I too felt hopelessly weak in the presence of the djinni. I remembered how Shalatan had pointed her finger at me, rendering me instantly unconscious. This was a different type of power, but one that was equally difficult to resist. It was nothing to do with courage; it was simply impossible to counter the force. The power of movement slowly began to desert me, and I lacked even the will to draw my sword or lift my shield. My knees began to buckle beneath me.

Other dark figures were now moving out of the shadows towards us: Hob's dark, cowled servants, whispering in harmony as they assembled behind their dread master. There were perhaps fifteen or twenty of these tassels, and they carried cruel curved blades that gleamed in that low light.

But then, with a terrible cry, Tyron threw back the second bolt and fell to his knees, struggling desperately with the third and final one, which was set close to the floor. This bolt was the longest and heaviest of all, running right across the great double doors.

I saw that Tyron lacked the strength to draw it back alone. I gritted my teeth and took a step towards him. But one step was all I could manage; I couldn't move again.

Now Hob was moving directly towards Tyron. The nearest of the tassels was almost upon me, raising its hooked blade to cut my throat.

Just when it seemed that we had failed and would die here, with an agonized groan, Tyron managed to draw back the third bolt, and immediately the doors began to open as if pushed by an invisible, giant hand. He rolled clear, and a shaft of moonlight was cast down between the doors like a great spear. And now it was the turn of Hob and his servants to halt; they stood immobile, as if rooted to the floor.

And suddenly a horse and rider straddled the threshold, bathed in moonlight. The horse reared up, its nostrils flaring, and steam formed a cloud about its head like dragon's breath. And above and beyond the rider, like a partial halo, I could see the sharp curve of the crescent moon; the phase known to the Genthai as the Wolf Moon.

At this apparition, Hob raised his hand to form a fist, which he pointed towards the door; a wave of terror seemed to radiate towards us, causing my knees to yield, and I fell forward. The horse reared up again and whinnied, but the rider controlled it and its hooves came down with a crash, throwing up sparks from the mosaic floor.

I looked up at the rider, and recognized the heavy moustache of the Genthai warrior – and the resolve in his eyes. Who else could it be but Konnit! He was always at the forefront of Genthai attacks: he had been first through the gate during the battle for the Protector's palace. But could he withstand Hob's terrible power?

Konnit urged his mount onwards. In his left hand he carried a torch that flickered against the colonnades and filled the hall with yellow light; in his right he raised his bright sword.

Horse and rider surged forward as one and, with one blow, Konnit struck hard and true at Hob's neck, severing the head. So powerful was the blow that the head went sailing through the air and landed amongst the pillars, to be lost in the deeper darkness there.

Three other mounted warriors – Donat, Kalasar and Tundar – now rode into the hall; and each, like Konnit, carried a torch and a sword. All four Genthai now attacked Hob's servants; servants who fled before them, their spirits broken. But they ran in vain, for they were pursued even amongst the pillars, the torches casting grotesque shadows as they screamed and died. And the Genthai archers beside me tried to take aim with their bows, but could find no certain target, so fast and furious was the slaughter.

Within minutes, no visible enemy still breathed within that hall, and the bodies of the fallen either lay inert or twitched in the agonies of death.

Then the remainder of our force entered the hall. First came Thrym, dressed for combat in Arena 13. He wore the same armour as us humans, hiding his throat-slit so that he looked like a warrior. His face looked grim but noble, and his glittering eyes were stern. The lacs behind him had great double-bladed battle-axes strapped to their shoulders and, slung between them on poles, carried a heavy cylindrical leather case. To these four had been trusted the gramagandar – the weapon upon which our victory would depend.

They set their load down on the tiles and stepped forward. Two of them tugged the axes from their shoulders, and there and then began to dismember Hob's carcass.

Tyron came to his feet slowly, releasing his breath with a great sigh; he reached out a hand and pulled me to my feet.

'Well, Leif, it was a close-run thing. Closer than I expected. For a moment there I thought we'd lost at the first throw . . .'

I just nodded. I felt drained of all strength and couldn't

speak. Tyron walked across towards the pillars on the left. He returned holding aloft Hob's bloody head. This he cast down onto the floor close to the mutilated body, and made a sign.

One of the lacs brought the axe down twice, cutting the head into four pieces. Tyron watched closely while this was done, then came back to join me.

'We do this for a purpose – not in malice,' he said. 'A djinni has great powers of regeneration. Each self must be dismembered and scattered as widely as possible. Burning is best, but we don't have time for that now.'

He made a gesture, and the pieces were taken outside to be scattered widely on the hillside. At the same time the four warriors returned their mounts to the keeping of those guarding the wagons. It was time to descend into the labyrinths beneath Hob's citadel; horses would be of no use there.

'Well,' said Tyron. 'First blood to us, but that was just one of Hob's selves. Now, as we begin our descent, we face an even greater danger.'

Thrym led the way, with Konnit at his shoulder and Tyron and me following close behind. Immediately to our rear, Kalasar, Tundar and Donat led the other Genthai warriors. Then came the lacs with their burden. We passed beyond the throne, down three steps from the dais, through an ornate bronze archway and into a circular chamber with a floor of polished white marble. From this chamber radiated five dark, narrow passages.

We followed Thrym into the central tunnel. At first it descended steeply, but soon levelled out. The going was firm, but there was a thin covering of dust; dust that rose in clouds about us as we walked. The walls radiated a soft yellow light, so we had no need for torches.

The tunnel curved to the left and we looked into a high, narrow chamber. In the rock wall on my left I saw three large recesses. Looking into the first, I recoiled – until I realized that this was a crypt and that its occupant had been dead for a long time. All that remained was a skeleton.

The dead creature had been perhaps seven or eight times the height of a man, and from its torso protruded several white appendages like thin branches; it was as if the bark had peeled away after the centre had rotted and the roots withered; yet they were still covered with very fine hair like down. They were jointed in four or five places, and from the tip of each protruded a cruel barbed nail that might have been a stinger. But these limbs seemed to have been carefully positioned so as to fit in the limited confines of the recess.

The huge skull lay in front of the body, and there were two dark holes in it – sockets that had once held the eyes.

'It's a shatek all right,' Tyron said. 'We're looking at the remains of a very old sycoda shatek. This beauty probably gave birth to Hob. Ada told me that the longer they live, the larger they grow. This abomination also gives birth to itself.

'Somewhere down here, a version or versions of that creature still live. That's what we've got to find and destroy. Hob doesn't simply regenerate; he can be born again and again.'

'How many shateks could there be? Shalatan numbered seven hundred and thirteen selves, but only one shatek. Surely Hob has far fewer selves – so how many shateks would he need?' I asked.

'Don't forget, Leif, that Hob is a rogue djinni,' Tyron told me. 'He's thrown off his original patterning and modified himself to meet his own needs. Kill Shalatan's lone shatek and she could no longer regenerate. It would take time, but it would be a death sentence. Hob is also an artificer of Nym and can use wurdes to pattern his future. I expect he has several shateks as an insurance policy in case one or more are killed.'

MY LORD IS MERCIFUL

When a human soul is clothed in false flesh, is it the
same or is it changed? Does it remember its past
life, or only think that it remembers?

Only Nym knows the truth.

The Manual of Nym

LEIF

Soon we were moving along narrow, claustrophobic tunnels;
these also radiated enough light to see clearly by. The going
was softer now, the clay tugging at our boots, and the four
lacs were snorting and bellowing like oxen as they struggled
along with the gramagandar.

We had moved Thrym to the back, to direct the lacs when
it came to firing the weapon. I stared back at it. It was
attached by leather straps to the poles, but the case had been
removed so that it was ready for action.

The gramagandar was cast from dark metal with a reddish
hue – a great cylinder with a bulbous end upon which was
superimposed the shape of a wolf's head; the lips were drawn

back in anger to reveal fangs, the mouth open to emit fiery breath.

The stem was long, about one and a half times the length of a man's body, and twice a man's waist in circumference – and strange forms were cast upon it, looking like distended veins; and I saw words in a language I didn't recognize, along with strange whorls and crisscrossing lines.

The tunnel brought us at last to a dark cavern, and we were all – apart from the four lacs burdened with the gramagandar – forced to light our torches and hold them aloft. Before us was an astonishing and terrifying sight.

Hundreds of large round grey things swayed in the darkness as if moved by the wind, even though the air was still and humid. They looked like mushrooms with very thin stalks. The cavern was full of them – row after row – almost as if they were being cultivated. There was a strong stench of rot, but it wasn't that which brought the bile rushing up my throat so that I struggled not to vomit.

I was not looking at fungi. They were severed human heads, swaying on long stems, each about shoulder-height. Their eyes were open and they were staring at us, their faces twitching in expressions of torment.

So this was what Hob did to those he took into his citadel. Tyron had bought back Kern's head and burned it so that it couldn't fall into Hob's evil hands again. But what was the purpose of this? Why keep these heads alive in such a dreadful fashion?

With a cry of grief, Tyron rushed forward and began to stare at the heads, moving through the rows as if searching for something. Was he looking for a friend who had been snatched by Hob and reduced to this? I wondered.

We formed a line beside those heads and watched silently as Tyron continued his search. After about ten minutes Konnit placed his hand on my shoulder.

'Go and bring him back, Leif. We can delay no longer.'

I passed through the rows of swaying heads, watching their eyes as they pleaded with me, mouths opening and closing silently. Perhaps they weren't all defeated combatants. Maybe some were ordinary citizens, snatched from the streets of Gindeen after dark, I thought. It seemed as if they were begging me for help. But how could they be helped – other than by doing what Tyron had done for Kern?

He had severed the tubes at the base of his neck, which allowed him to descend into the peace of death. Should we put these poor tormented souls out of their misery as well? It would surely be a kindness.

I reached Tyron just as he was checking the last row, staring closely into each poor face.

'We need to move on,' I said softly.

'Yes, yes,' he said, bowing his head and staring at his boots.

'Were you looking for a friend?' I asked.

He looked up and met my eyes. 'I was looking for a friend, but she isn't here,' he said. 'I had to be sure. You're right – we've delayed too long. We must move on.'

'Before we go, should we give them peace?' I asked.

Tyron met my gaze, but then he shook his head. 'If we succeed, there'll be no need for that. If we fail, then we may share their fate.'

Without any further explanation, he gave me a curt nod and then led the way back to join the others.

Within minutes we'd reached the cavern's far wall, and again we entered a tunnel that led to another cavern, so high and so vast that, despite our torches, its roof was lost in darkness.

The first warning of danger was nothing more than a faint trembling in the air. Suddenly there was an ominous whistling, and then a shower of deadly arrows fell amongst us while, ahead, a blinding light, brighter than a thousand torches, was directed on us.

Whether it was meant to blind us or to illuminate us in order to aid those who opposed us, I do not know. Out of its glare monstrous, distorted shapes moved towards us; human in form, yet with legs that were too long and arms that had too many joints. They reared up before us, an army of Hob's deadly selves. What chance had mere humans against such entities?

Amongst those forms were others, closer in size to men, which wore armour and brandished swords. Were these servants of Hob or his selves in different forms? Certainly, there were some servants – I could see hooded tassels there too, some running towards us on all fours.

My heart hammered in my chest as I felt a surge of excitement and fear. This was the battle we had anticipated. This would pose a far greater threat than the one we had faced in the throne room. Instead of just one self and a few tassels, we were now up against myriad selves and an army of servants.

We were so few. How could we hope to prevail here? So much depended upon the gramagandar, I thought. Had the Genthai ever tested it – and, if so, against what? Konnit had said nothing about this. No doubt the weapon was very old, perhaps dating from before the fall of the Human Empire. Would it still be effective? I wondered. Perhaps the djinn had developed some means of countering its threat? Perhaps that was the function of the bright light?

And then another volley of arrows hailed down upon us. On my left I saw one embed itself deeply in Brid's neck; he threw up his hands and collapsed, then lay convulsing at our feet.

I fell to my knees, stunned and unable to think, holding my shield above my head. And all about me, others were doing likewise, seeking to avoid the deadly shower that sought to take our lives. Our own archers hadn't yet managed to fire a single arrow in return.

I looked back. Only Thrym and the four lacs bearing the gramagandar were still on their feet.

But then Konnit leaped up, a weapon in each hand. His face was contorted with fury and he was mouthing something, shouting words that were wild and unintelligible. We were all rising to our feet now, and Konnit was already running towards the light.

As one, we began a desperate charge, our archers now wielding blades, and I ran with them, my own sense of self lost within the common purpose. As I did so, it was as if, deep within my mind, I could hear the howl of a wolf. It seemed to me that I was not just a warrior running with other Genthai to face a common enemy. I was a wolf running with its pack, seeking to tear the flesh of its enemies. And it didn't matter that the enemy outnumbered us by at least five to one.

In my right hand I held the short sword; in my left the

circular shield. As we collided with the first ranks of our enemies, I felt something reach for me from the right and struck out with my blade; it met a solid shape, and I staggered, then regained my balance and ran on. I sliced right and left with both sword and shield, but soon the massed ranks we faced grew too great and I was being pressed on three sides.

I turned and saw that others were fighting beside me. On my right Konnit, a huge sword in each hand, was hacking to and fro with great blows so that the enemy fell like trees before him; on my left Kalasar was finding flesh with every quick thrust and cut.

However, now the light that shone into our eyes waxed even brighter; we were partially blinded and, as one foe fell, another sprang forward to replace it. Some were terrible indeed – far taller than men, their arms almost out of reach.

There were too many – far too many – and soon my strength began to fail. I was forced to give ground, along with those who fought at my side.

But then I heard a sound behind me; a vibration that set my teeth on edge. And suddenly, with a cough and a roar, the flame of the gramagandar seared out towards us.

Even in the heat of battle I glanced back and saw that terrible tongue of purple fire surging towards the very point where we fought. It was supposed to destroy only false flesh, but surely nothing that lived could endure the intensity of such a flame?

For a moment I was distracted and one creature sliced down at my unprotected head. I brought up my shield too late to parry that blow and knew that I was as good as dead.

But I never felt it; instead I saw my attacker crumple before me. All around us, our enemies staggered and fell or tried to run, and the bright light began to dim like dusk following the setting sun. I saw flesh melt from faces, bones bend, eyes bubble and flow out of their sockets, limbs contort and break as the gramagandar did its deadly work.

The flame reached out towards me again, the purple punctuated by pulses of darkness and juddering roars; but that tongue of fire licked through and past my own flesh as if it was not there. When it reached our enemies, however, its effect was lethal, their armour crumpling and twisting upon bodies that dissolved within.

All those clothed in false flesh died; those that remained, the tassels, scampered away with whimpering cries, scurrying off like rats into the darkness.

As one, we turned our backs on the dying and headed back towards that terrible fire. The four lacs, grimacing under the strain of its great weight, were now angling the flame upwards. At their backs, Thrym kept well away lest he too be destroyed.

I looked up, following the weapon's trajectory, and saw the enemy archers standing high above us, hidden until that moment by darkness. Our own archers began to fire on them, now they were illuminated by the purple flame of the Wolf's breath. They tried to escape along the high ledge, some allowing their weapons to fall, some falling themselves even before the tongue of fire reached their flesh. And their cries were shrill upon the air as they dropped into the darkness, but the gramagandar breathed its fire along that ledge until nothing moved there.

Its job done for now, the deadly weapon was fitted with

carrying straps once more. But as the lacs prepared to take up their burden, Tyron motioned them to wait.

Oil was poured upon the body of the fallen Brid, and a torch used to set it alight. His comrades watched silently as Tyron performed this kindness. We had no certainty of victory, and if we should be forced to retreat, he wanted to keep the remains of his friend safe from Hob.

Meanwhile Konnit spoke quietly to me. 'Did you feel it?' he asked. 'It was with us. *The Wolf was with us.*'

There was a religious fervour to his voice; it sounded hoarse and wavered as if it was not fully under control.

'I felt it,' I admitted. 'I heard it howl within my head.'

We fell silent while the body of poor Brid burned, our nostrils filled with the stench of burning meat. Then I looked at Konnit again.

'I know that the gramagandar is supposed to be harmless to human flesh, but I thought my last moment had come. I thought it would consume us too,' I admitted.

He smiled grimly. 'The weapon is designed to destroy all false flesh; all those born of a shatek must fall before it. That's why I prevented Ada from joining us here. However, even true flesh may, in time, suffer as a result of its touch. Old age may be more painful, bones become more brittle, weakness come faster. But that is of little concern to us now. Don't worry, Leif – we are warriors and need not fear old age.'

We continued our journey, our progress still slow. We were descending towards the deepest part of this system of caverns and tunnels. Tyron believed that far below we would find the shateks that enabled Hob to create new selves. There we would destroy them.

Some of the torches had been lost in the battle, but enough remained to light our way; we were ever vigilant, but saw no sign of our enemy, nor of those who did his bidding.

Sometimes we trudged along what seemed to be new tunnels, which were soft underfoot, slowing us down even further. But, increasingly, we followed ancient tunnels paved with loose stone chips linking caverns of various sizes. The caverns were created by the effects of water and other natural forces, but the tunnels had been cut by Hob and those who served him. These caverns now dripped with water, and occasionally small streams flowed across our path or meandered alongside before falling into some dark abyss.

We came at last to a cavern where a wall of water fell sheer out of the darkness, pouring into a deep basin, where it sent up a great cloud of spray and filled the air with thunder. Within that basin the water swirled widdershins before hurtling across great boulders, then down another great cascade into the darkness.

As we approached the tumult, our torchlight showed a slender figure waiting at its edge; the form of a woman with long fair hair blown upwards by the turbulence.

I was astonished. Was she someone Hob had snatched from the streets and kept alive? I wondered.

But, seeing her, Tyron let out a groan, as if he was in pain, and made his way to the front, signalling for everyone else to stay back. Sensing danger, I followed at his heels and, as he approached the woman, caught his arm.

'Who is it? Is it someone you knew?' I asked.

Tyron's eyes were wild in the torchlight, and I saw tears of grief glistening on his cheeks; grief growing to a torrent that threatened to overwhelm him.

'Aye, it's someone I knew once, Leif. Someone worth more to me than even life itself. Her name was Jacanda, and she was the mother of Teena and Kwin. She was my wife – until Hob took her for his own.'

Tyron had never spoken of her, and I had never questioned him. She had died of a fever when Kwin was hardly more than a baby, I had been told. Now, suddenly, much was clear. Tyron had kept a secret even from his own children – for Hob had slain Jacanda.

With a shudder, he tore himself free of my grip and began to walk swiftly towards the woman. This cavern was dimly lit, so I seized a torch from Kalasar and ran forward until I drew level with him. We halted together before the woman.

'I have a message for you, Tyron,' the woman said; 'a message from my lord.' Her voice was hoarse and filled with pain; it was hard to hear it clearly above the roar of falling water.

Even in the torchlight, the flame agitated by the turbulence, the evidence of Hob's abuse was beyond doubt: Jacanda's throat was horribly swollen, and dark bruises marked her arms and legs. The sides of her mouth had been ripped open – that or slit by a blade – and fresh blood ran in two rivulets down her neck to darken the white gown she clasped to her throat.

Tyron groaned and held out his arms towards her. He tried to speak but, when he opened his mouth, no words came out.

The woman was young; very young – surely the soul of

Tyron's wife clothed in false flesh and born of a shatek. In her left earlobe was a small silver earring in the form of a wolf. I suddenly realized that she looked just like Kwin.

'My lord asks me to tell you that it is not too late for you to beg his forgiveness. If you turn back, he will give you two great gifts.'

'Gifts?' Tyron asked, taking a step closer.

'Firstly, he will let our two daughters live out their lives in the world above unmolested. Secondly, he will allow me to return with you so that we four can once more be together.'

Tyron shook his head and started to turn away, but she suddenly stepped forward and grasped his arm.

'Oh, Tyron!' she cried. 'My lord is merciful. Just do what he asks and we can be happy again. Please. Please . . . I've missed you so terribly and the pain is so hard to bear. It was always you I loved. Always you.'

Again, Tyron started to turn and reached down to move her hand off his arm. And, in that second, I saw what was going to happen. But all my speed and skill availed me nothing. I had time to take just one futile step.

And it was already too late . . .

Jacanda leaped over the edge of the pool, still holding onto Tyron's arm. He staggered and tried to regain his balance, but then toppled with her into the abyss.

Whether they cried out it was impossible to say. All sound was drowned out by the thunder of the waterfall. I glanced down and saw the bodies of Tyron and Jacanda strike the rocks; there was a brief spatter of red before they were borne swiftly away into the darkness.

THE BREATH OF THE WOLF

It is little wonder that the djinn hated and feared
the gramagandar. Little wonder too that humans
deployed it without mercy.

If a weapon exists, it will be used.

But there are always consequences.

The History of the Conflict by Eitel the Pessimist

LEIF

I was shocked to my core. My mind in a whirl, I sat down on
the damp rocks and buried my face in my hands while the
roar of the cascade filled my ears.

A crazy thought whirled through my head even faster than
the vortex of water swirling in the rocky basin at the foot of
the waterfall: Tyron might still be alive!

I leaped to my feet, about to dive into the maelstrom and
rescue him. I even opened my mouth to shout out for help,
but then I remembered the long fall and the splash of red
blood on the rocks, and knew that Tyron was gone for ever.

It had happened so quickly. If only I'd stepped between him
and the woman. Now it was too late, and I could only rock

back and forth on my heels, seeing that terrible image over and over again. I sat down again, and at one point someone came and shouted into my left ear, but I pushed them away.

I became aware that the others were setting down their burdens and squatting on the ground some distance away, but it seemed unimportant. Whatever happened now, it no longer mattered. Nothing could change what had taken place. I was filled with a terrible grief and sense of loss.

Tyron had been my trainer and my friend. Long ago I had lost my father, Math; this was like losing a father all over again. Tyron had guided and advised me; he had helped to make me what I was. Now poor Teena had lost her husband, father and mother to Hob. How would her frail mind be able to cope with the grief? How could I ever tell her the truth of what had just happened? And Kwin . . . Despite their arguments, she had loved her father deeply.

For a long time I lingered beside the waterfall, my mind numb. Then I looked up and saw Thrym standing silently at my side, with Konnit close by.

'We need to press on now,' Konnit said.

But before I could reply, Thrym spoke. 'What is your will, Leif?' he asked.

'My will . . .' I mused, shaking my head, still in shock. 'For so long now my will has been the will of Tyron – I can't believe he's gone. I just want to complete what he started.'

'Then listen to me,' Thrym said. 'Listen well. You know what must be done. We must take the weapon to the place where the mothers of Hob still dwell. We must find and destroy those shateks – though many of our enemies stand between us and that place. In order to breach their defence, we must use the gramagandar again.'

I nodded grimly. 'Whatever it takes. We can't turn back now.'

Now Konnit came to kneel at my side. 'Once we have reached the place of the shateks, a second thing must be done,' he said grimly. 'The gramagandar is a weapon that works in two ways. The first you have already seen. In the second, the Breath of the Wolf is released slowly, in expand-ing waves of death. It slowly exhales three times, each breath reaching out further than the last. A shatek and all born of her flesh will die at its touch.'

'Then you too will die,' I said, gazing directly into Thrym's eyes.

'All born of a shatek must die here,' he replied. 'There will be a long pause between each breath, but the third will reach up to the world above. It will pass through rock and cleanse both the underworld and the towers and spires and extend to the edge of the city. If I am able to, I'll leave before this last lethal breath.'

'Why can't Thrym leave us immediately so that we can start this here and now?' I demanded of Konnit. 'We must be close to the shateks. Couldn't the gramagandar destroy them from here?'

'Perhaps, but there would be no certainty of success,' he told me. 'We must reach their lair, their birthing chambers. Only by placing the gramagandar there can we be truly cer-tain of destroying them.'

'Then we've no choice. We must go on,' I said, getting to my feet and retrieving my sword and shield.

*

At last we entered a cavern so vast that it might have accommodated the Wheel itself.

Here the light was faint and we'd only a few torches remaining, so there was much that might lie hidden in the shadows. Then, far ahead, across the cavern, lit from behind by an arc of light, I saw our enemies arrayed against us: a band of Hob's selves, several score strong. This time there was no bright light to turn them into silhouettes and obscure their faces. And I saw that their faces were all the same!

Each large hairless head had a hooked nose and strange, terrifying eyes, the small dark iris lost within the expanse of white eyeball. And every one of those faces that glared at us, emanating power and hatred, was the face of Hob.

Beyond these, glowing and shimmering in the darkness, stood a bridge that curved in a great iridescent arc over a black chasm, as if linking two shores. But the further shore was lost in mist, and at first I took that bridge to be a trick of the light, an ethereal projection upon which no creature of substance could ever safely step.

But Thrym pointed directly at it. 'I suspect that the shateks sleep beyond that bridge. We must cross to the far side and search for them.'

I looked again at our foe. A few of the warriors that looked like Hob were dressed as if for Arena 13, in the leather shorts and short-sleeved jerkins that left their flesh bare for the blade. Others wore dark armour, with helmets that obscured their faces, and wielded longswords or great axes; some even carried spears.

They might not all be selves of Hob, I reflected. Were some of these the dead, or those who, through fear, obeyed a terrible master? I thought again of Jacanda, who had taken Tyron to his death; the husband she had professed to love even as she prepared to end his life.

Why? Was it because Hob had promised to leave their daughters alone? Was it to save Teena and Kwin from the torments of this underworld?

Then another terrible thought slid into my mind. Tyron had fallen – almost certainly to his death. But what if Hob managed to retrieve his head and animate it, thus adding it to those tormented souls we had already seen? That must not be allowed to happen. That was one more reason to obliterate Hob entirely.

We needed to slay all these who opposed us. Some might indeed be poor suffering beings who were also victims . . . But we had no choice.

'Stand aside!' cried Konnit, calling to our enemies. 'Stand aside and let us pass! Stand aside or feel the wrath of the Genthai!'

But his words sounded empty; they echoed back off the walls and were distorted, falling away into nothingness. For death in this place had no meaning for the followers of Hob. A djinni did not die as humans died. Those selves didn't fear us. They only sought to protect the shateks, which promised immortality. Their individual deaths meant nothing.

As for the others who served Hob here, why should they care for our threats? The only certainty they knew was the torment their dark lord inflicted on them; his will was all.

The assembled ranks quickly gave their answer: laughter rippled out across the cavern – a laughter that grew and grew into a thunder of contempt. Then, as it faded, they clanged swords against shields or struck boots or weapons on the ground – metal, wood or leather upon stone – so that the cavern rang and boomed with the tumult of their challenge.

And then they charged.

Even before he spoke Konnit had nodded to Thrym: the gramagandar was already in position. With a cough and a deep roar, the Breath of the Wolf spread out to sear our enemies. Many fell immediately, licked into swift dissolution by that purple tongue of fire; others ran on a little way before they too staggered and fell.

A few avoided those pulses of fire and came at us from the side. But we formed a defensive circle around the weapon and, even as they attacked, Konnit began to lead us towards the bridge, moving forward as rapidly as the lacs who carried the weapon could manage.

Very few of our enemies reached that defensive ring, but those that did were cut down by Genthai blades and arrows; and, under the direction of Thrym, the four lacs turned slowly clockwise so that the gramagandar pulsed fire in a great circle. And I felt the vibration in my teeth as that fire passed through me. I remembered Konnit's words:

We are warriors and need not fear old age.

But now we had reached the bridge and, with the gramagandar pointing backwards to destroy any pursuers, Thrym took the lead and began the long climb to its apex, which soared over a deep, dark chasm.

I followed him, but no sooner had I set foot upon the bridge than a warm wind blasted upwards from the darkness below; a gale that roared about my ears and stank of rotting seaweed cast up onto a mudflat. It was the stench of stagnant seawater into which flesh had decayed, the putrefaction of a dead womb.

Despite this, I did not falter, and moments later the air was still again, and I could hear footsteps echoing back from the stony vault far above. I looked behind and saw Konnit and Kalasar following in my wake and, further back, the four lacs struggling with their heavy burden. Behind them came Tundar and the five Genthai archers, who were still firing at our pursuers.

The bridge under my feet was translucent, like crystal, but felt abrasive and coarse. The incline became steeper and, as we approached the apex, it suddenly became slippery underfoot; I stumbled and almost fell. Fear of that great chasm beneath me made me slow my pace.

And the thought came to me that, with one wrong step, the four lacs carrying the gramagandar could send all hope plunging into the abyss. Yet the bridge was wider than it had looked, and keeping to its centre we hoped that we were safe.

It was then that I saw three dark armoured figures waiting right at the centre of the bridge. Were these the last selves of Hob? I wondered.

Thrym turned and spoke. 'Leave them to me, Leif,' he said in a voice that was more command than request. He drew his blades.

'No,' Konnit said. 'Why take a risk when there is a far easier way?'

At that Thrym smiled grimly and the gramagandar was brought forward. Its flame quickly cleared the bridge of opposition.

Was that almost the end of Hob? Surely all that remained

now were the shateks, the mothers who might yet regenerate his selves?

The wind came again from the pit, filling my nostrils with its stench, this time almost extinguishing our remaining torches.

Thrym and I reached the top of the bridge and began the descent, walking side by side. We saw that this side extended right down into what appeared to be a roughly circular crater. The high inner walls of this vast pit were dimly lit, the light that radiated from the rainbow bridge itself brighter by far. But as we descended, both sources of light began to wane, and after another two dozen paces we slowed and, in the deepening gloom, waited for the gramagandar, and then Konnit and Kalasar. Immediately behind them were two of the archers, but Tundar and the others had remained in the centre of the bridge to guard our rear.

Konnit was carrying a torch, so he moved into the lead with Thrym, while I followed behind them with the others. At last we reached the end of the bridge; around us was darkness, and our torches cast huge distorted shadows onto the circular wall that enclosed us. Now we could see caverns at the base of this wall – thirteen dark, hungry mouths, each of which could be home to a shatek. However, we had to be sure.

Suddenly I heard a sound – a series of light clicks like the flexing of ancient bones, coming from the mouth of the nearest tunnel. Then a head slowly emerged into the light – a bestial head, a travesty of the human female, smooth and devoid of hair, with eyes that were large, luminous and green.

Yes, this was indeed the lair of the shateks!

Already the lacs had set the weapon down on the ground;

two were positioning it while two had pulled the double-bladed axes from their backs and stood facing the shatek.

I studied the creature more carefully: its nose was large and its mouth was open, the voluptuous lips pulled back to reveal double rows of teeth, sharp and curving back towards the dark throat like the poisonous fangs of a serpent. But any resemblance to a human female ended there, for the body that scuttled into the flickering torchlight was similar to that of the shatek Ada had bought from the Trader; similar also to the shatek of Shalatan. Its glistening black body was like that of an insect, but it had eight legs and was twice the size of an ox – far bigger than either of the two I'd seen previously.

Now it darted out of the cave, running straight towards us. But the two lacs raised their axes high and brought them down on its head. The first blow was deflected, as if by armour, but the second bit deep into the shatek's left eye. It screamed in agony and retreated back towards the tunnel, shaking its head and splattering its attackers with gore. Then, suddenly, it turned, raised its head and vomited, projecting towards its attackers a long silver arc of fluid.

Now it was the turn of the lacs to scream: both fell to their knees, clutching their faces. Steam rose from their unprotected heads and I realized that the fluid was burning their skin and eyes.

The shatek was rushing towards us again, but an arrow had buried itself in the remaining eye and it came to a halt, shaking its head from side to side, as if to dislodge it. From a cave to our left emerged another shatek, and this one too was stopped by an arrow. More shateks were appearing, but

Konnit shouted at the three archers on the bridge, who came running to help their comrades. They now proved their worth, for again and again they fired with deadly accuracy, their arrows finding their targets: the shateks were hit or forced to withdraw back into the safety of their lairs.

The immediate danger seemed to be over.

'How long will it take? How long before the first breath is released?' I asked Konnit.

'In less than a minute it will be ready,' he replied.

'And the second?'

'An hour. And the third a further hour after that.'

'Then run, Thrym. Run for your life!' I commanded. 'Return to the surface.'

'But there is still danger here,' he protested.

'Listen, Thrym. One day we may face a greater enemy even than Hob. Run swiftly, I command you. Save yourself for that.'

He turned obediently, ran past the gramagandar and was soon lost to sight over the bridge. Some of our enemies had pursued us to the other side, but how many and whether they could halt Thrym was difficult to say. I worried that he wouldn't have time to escape the first exhalation of the Wolf.

And, indeed, the Wolf soon breathed out. The first warning was a tingling in my teeth; a discomfort that quickly became a pain; and immediately the gramagandar began to glow with a soft orange light.

For a moment I felt dizzy; then I felt weak – and then came a brief flash of light so intense that I was temporarily blinded.

When I could see again, I hurried past the gramagandar, averting my eyes from the lacs who'd collapsed across it; lacs who had laboured hard to bring to this place the instrument of their own destruction. In the tunnels, Hob's shateks must also be dead, I knew.

We had won. Surely Hob was no more. My vengeance was complete, and the people of Midgard were finally safe from that cruel predator. It was good to taste victory after so long, but now we needed to escape from Hob's lair. There might still be bands of tassels untouched by the gramagandar.

Konnit gestured towards the bridge, and we made our way carefully across that slippery surface, speeding up as the going grew easier on the other side. On our way out of the citadel we might encounter tassels, but there was no desperate need for haste, and we proceeded through the tunnels and caverns at a steady pace. At the beginning of the second hour, the Wolf, now left behind us, breathed out for a second time, and the few enemies we saw had already started to dissolve.

At last we reached the place where the human heads had swayed on stalks, silently pleading to us. There we halted briefly, amazed by the change wrought by the breath of the gramagandar.

The heads were intact, but now they lay on the ground, their open eyes unseeing in death. It was the stems formed of false flesh that had melted or withered, denying sustenance to those poor tortured humans. It was a merciful release from what Hob had inflicted upon them.

We continued on towards the surface. Despite our victory I felt strangely uneasy; gradually this grew into a strong sense of foreboding.

What if beyond the citadel, out of reach of the final breath of the gramagandar, one of Hob's selves had escaped destruction? Wode and his men were guarding the Wheel and the area around it, but they couldn't watch everything. One of his selves might have been out there spying – perhaps even working within the Wheel itself. If this was the case, it would exact a terrible revenge for what had been done here.

I began to walk faster. I wanted to be sure that Kwin was safe, but my heart was heavy with the burden I carried towards her.

I would have to tell her of the death of her father.

MY NAME IS KWIN

Look into a mirror and speak. If you recognize your
reflection, you are sentient.

But where does your consciousness reside?

Within your head or within its reflection?

The Manual of Nym

KWIN

I'd stayed in the admin building longer than usual. As the
start of the season approached, there was much more to do
and I had to keep on top of the paperwork.

It was a good excuse too. I didn't want to be around while
my father and Leif made their preparations to attack Hob. It
would only have made me more anxious. So I had said my
farewells at breakfast and spent the day working hard to
keep my fears at bay.

Thrym was going to be part of the attack, so I had a sub-
stitute guard, a young Genthai warrior who'd forgotten how
to smile. Sternly, and with his back ramrod straight, he
escorted me home through the gloomy city streets. When I

approached the house, it was already dark. I thanked him, and he nodded in return and left me at the entrance to the yard.

The usual lights shone in the windows, but I sensed the emptiness even before I unlocked the door. Three of my father's servants should have been on the premises – the cook to prepare the evening meal and the two armed guards who were always in attendance after dark. I knew that Teena and her son were spending the night at the Respite House, but Deinon and Ada should also have been home.

I went into the kitchen – to be greeted with silence. Unnerved, I called out loudly, 'Ada! Deinon! I'm home!'

There was no reply.

A stew was simmering on the stove, but there was no sign of the cook. I went upstairs and knocked on the door of the bedroom Deinon shared with Leif – the long room that, until those two became permanent residents, my father had always given his youngest trainees. There was no reply, so I eased open the door. The room was empty.

I went to Ada's room. That was empty too. Now I was becoming anxious. I looked through the window, down onto the yard, and drew in a sharp breath. Something was moving in the darkness.

At that moment the moon came out from behind a cloud to illuminate a cloaked figure crawling slowly across the flags, heading for the back door.

It was a tassel – one of Hob's servants. They were cannibals and killers. Did it intend to enter the house? I wondered.

I allowed my blade to slip down my sleeve into my left hand and listened carefully as it halted with its forehead almost touching the door. What was it doing? Was it trying to break in?

To my surprise, the tassel turned and crawled away from the door, heading towards the far wall of the yard. Then the moon was covered by cloud again, and I could see it no more.

Holding the knife, I crept slowly downstairs, not knowing what to expect. Then I saw a sheet of paper on the floor. It had been pushed under the door.

I carried it to the light of the nearest candle and examined the writing. It was crude, and appeared to have been scrawled in blood.

> *Ada is my prisoner. I offer her one chance of life. Come to the Wheel tonight and face me in Arena 13. She will be my target. You will defend her. If you refuse to fight, I will cause her extreme and prolonged pain before I finally slit her throat.*

I knew that Hob often lied and realized that Ada might already be dead.

But I couldn't assume this. I had to go. I had no choice.

I am preparing to fight Hob.

I will do so in the hope of saving Ada's life.

I begin my ritual. I stare at my face in the mirror and concentrate. I mouth the first command:

'*Paint it black!*'

The girl in the mirror obeys immediately, tracing the contour of her top lip with swift, precise strokes.

I mouth the second command:

'*Paint it red!*'

Once more my reflection in the mirror obeys, painting her bottom lip the rich red of arterial blood.

I scowl so that the girl in the mirror looks fierce.

Her dark hair is longer on one side, reaching down to the edge of her jaw; on the other it barely reaches her eyebrow, which means that the scar is clearly visible. It is a thin diagonal line that extends from just below the left eye to the edge of the mouth.

I am already wearing the traditional Arena 13 shorts and jerkin, so that my arms and legs are bare, ready to be cut. Now I move away from the mirror and sit on the bed, reaching down to pick up my left boot. It must always be the left boot first. I tug it on and begin to lace it up. I tie a triple knot. Now it is the turn of the right boot. Once again I finish with a triple knot.

These are the special red Trig boots that Leif bought for me. They are the same colour as Hob's blood.

It is now time to ask the important question. I face the mirror again and lean forward so that my forehead is almost touching it. Then I speak:

'Girl in the mirror on the wall,

Who is the fastest of them all?'

She stares back at me and we mouth a single word in unison:

'Kwin!'

Once again, the ritual is complete, and now we are one.

I am Kwin, and I am ready to fight my enemy.

I left the house and crossed the city alone, hastening through the dark streets. None of the lanterns were lit – Gindeen was deserted. People were cowering behind bolted doors, fearing reprisals. The attack on Hob's lair was supposed to be a secret, but secrets are difficult to keep in this city.

I feared for Leif and my father. They were down in the tunnels deep below the citadel. I wondered if they had slain Hob's other selves? Or had Hob triumphed? Were they already dead?

But Hob had threatened to kill me in front of Leif. A truly dark thought entered my head. Perhaps the attack had failed and Leif was already his prisoner. I pushed the thought out of my mind and hurried on towards the Wheel, through the streets of a city lit with the silver light of the horned moon.

At last its wooden mass reared up above the surrounding houses, obscuring the stars and moon. The last people had long since left the building. I let myself in with my father's keys. The place was not in total darkness: a few torches were still lit so I could find my way to Arena 13.

I went down under the spectators' gallery and entered the Green Room. Here I saw a body lying next to the table. I approached it slowly, my heart racing, hardly daring to look in case it was my father or Leif.

It was neither of them, but it was somebody I knew.

The dead man was Wode, an artificer who had been my father's friend ever since they'd trained together as boys. His neck was broken, and the sight of his open, staring eyes reminded me of what had happened in the museum – the moment when the lights came back on and I found Goodwin dead at my feet.

Shuddering, I took a deep breath to calm myself and headed

for the far door. Beyond it, a short corridor led to the arena itself.

Here I saw another body, and this time I let out a wail of grief; tears began to run down my cheeks.

For I saw that it was poor Deinon.

His had not been the quick death meted out to Goodwin and Wode. Kneeling down beside him, I saw that his face was contorted with pain, the front of his shirt covered in blood, which pooled around his body. Now I realized that his fingers had been broken and were twisted at impossible angles.

Time seemed to stop as I stared down at him. He'd had such promise, such talent. He would have become one of the greatest patterners the city had ever seen. Leif and Deinon were close friends. If Leif survived, I'd have to break the terrible news to him.

Now I thought of Ada, who I hoped was still alive, and tore my gaze away. I got to my feet. Once again my whole body was trembling. I stepped round the body, avoiding the pool of blood.

The min door was open, so I moved cautiously into the arena, drawing the two Trigladius blades from the sheaths at my belt. There was no sign of Hob, and the large mag door was closed.

But Ada was there – and she was alive! She stood with her back to the far wall, staring at me.

She was dressed for combat in Arena 13, clad in the traditional leather shorts and jerkin so that, like mine, her flesh was open to the blade. She wore black Trigladius boots too. But the lower part of her face was fitted with a brown leather mask. It was moulded tightly to her flesh so that she was unable to speak words of Nym to our enemy.

Tears started to stream down her cheeks. For a moment I thought she was afraid of what she was about to face, but then I realized the truth: she already knew that Deinon was dead. She had liked the boy and they had grown close as she trained him in the use of Nym. Hob had made her witness his death.

My first thought was to remove the mask so that Ada could speak. I moved closer and raised a blade towards her, wondering how to cut it away without injuring her.

However, before I could do anything, her eyes widened in fear and I heard the deep rumble of the mag door.

I turned as Hob stepped through into the arena.

His huge figure was shrouded in darkness. This was the creature feared by everyone in Gindeen: the bogeyman that children were warned against. He filled their nightmares with horror. His shadow moved across cot and bed. He lurked within wardrobes, stared up at windows and sent shudders through the night.

A terrible unreasoning fear filled me, making my heart pound so that I gasped for breath and felt faint. The arena spun about me and darkness grew in the corners of my eyes.

I took a deep breath and focused upon what had to be done. Once more I recited the words of the ritual in my head:

Girl in the mirror on the wall,
Who is the fastest of them all?
'Kwin!'

My heart thudded with a deeper and steadier rhythm as

both doors began to close. Far above, the thirteen-branched candelabrum flared and started to descend. Now the arena was flooded with light. I stared at my enemy and moved between him and Ada.

Hob was also dressed for the arena, but he wasn't wearing his usual bronze mask. His head was larger than that of a man and was completely bald. His nose was hooked, like the beak of a predatory bird. But it was his eyes that drew my attention. There were large areas of white below the dark pupils, and as he stared unblinkingly at me, my legs suddenly felt weak.

I remembered what Leif had told me about their contest – how Hob had exerted some strange power so that Leif had felt powerless, in thrall to the djinni's will. I attempted to look away, but it was difficult. His eyes were fixed on mine. With a supreme effort, I broke the connection, staring instead at his mouth.

It was then that Hob spoke.

'Your father is dead, though the boy you love still lives.'

Tears sprang to my eyes. Hob *could* have been lying, but something told me that this was the truth. I felt a tremendous sense of loss, which threatened to overwhelm me.

'That is why I have summoned you here,' Hob continued. 'I intend to kill you – and the woman who stands behind you. I will do it slowly. Piece by piece I will cut away your flesh until you are almost unrecognizable as human beings. The woman tried to destroy me, and for that she will die. But my purpose in killing you is different. I want the boy, Leif, to see what I have done to you. When he arrives, despite your terrible injuries, you will still be breathing, still be conscious. I want him to hear you plead for death. I made him a promise long ago, and now I intend to keep it.'

He drew his blades from the scabbards at his hips and took a step towards me. I raised my own blades, ready to defend myself.

He towered over me, and I felt very small.

Hob paused, and the expression on his face was difficult to read. It was a mixture of contempt and hatred.

'The boy has changed since our first encounter,' he said gloatingly. 'He dared to threaten me and I was about to slay him on the spot. He sought revenge for the deaths of the humans who begat him. He was ready to die. Ready to sacrifice his own life in a hopeless attempt upon mine. But I saw how I might punish him. "Whom do you love?" I demanded, and he admitted that he had friends but loved no one. I saw that, like most humans, he would one day be subject to this weakness – he would love someone. I knew that if I were to kill the one he loved, it would hurt him more than death itself. You are now the object of his love, and that is why you are about to die.'

Without warning, Hob took two rapid steps towards me and lunged with the blade in his right hand. I wasn't fast enough to avoid it completely, but instead of cutting my shoulder to the bone, it sliced away only a small piece of flesh.

The pain seared through me, but I danced away, blood trickling down my arm, aware that Ada was moving with me, keeping me between her and Hob.

Having to defend Ada worried me. She was the greatest patterner who ever lived, so adept that, had it not been for the intervention of the Protector's Guard, her wurdes would have destroyed all Hob's selves. But she wasn't trained to fight in Arena 13. She knew the patterns of the combat dance, but wasn't practised in executing them herself.

I was slim and fit, my body perfectly honed for combat here. And I was very fast – faster than Leif, although I wouldn't say this to his face. But Ada carried more weight than me. She would struggle to dance close to my back, as she had to. So I would be forced to avoid Hob's blades while, at the same time, defending Ada.

Even without that, I think it would have been difficult to triumph over him.

Hob attacked again, and I moved backwards rapidly, bumping into Ada. At least she had anticipated my sudden retreat, and we managed to recover from that momentary clumsiness. Even better, I reacted quickly enough to strike Hob, cutting him on his left forearm. It was nothing – a minor wound – but it boosted my confidence. I was fast enough to cut Hob, but next time the cut had to be deeper.

I danced away to the right, retreating towards the wall of the arena. I could hear Ada moving close behind me. So far, so good.

Now Hob attacked me with both blades, but I avoided them.

Again I cut him – this time on the other arm; again the wound was minor, but it showed what I was capable of.

Could Hob know fear? I wondered. Would he be concerned by what I had already achieved? Could he imagine losing, even dying, at my hand?

But now, suddenly, he attacked again, pressing me back. I

could hear Ada breathing heavily. The longer I was forced to defend her, the more difficult it would be for her to stay safely in position behind me.

We were hard against the wall now. Ada must have been touching it. I drummed with my boots on the boards of the arena, using the sound-code Ulum, signalling to her the move I was about to make. It was fortunate that she'd worked with me in training. Each code was private, known only to a combatant and the lac or lacs working for them. An opponent didn't know what was being signalled.

Together we danced away to the left, but Ada was slower than me. I tried to protect her by blocking Hob's blades, but I was only partially successful.

I heard a muffled cry of pain and, as we danced clear and returned to the relative safety of the centre of the arena, I glanced back. There was blood trickling from Ada's finger-tips, and I saw a cut on her forearm – though it didn't look too serious. Fortunately Hob had missed the artery.

He came at me again, but I held my ground, blocking his blades and then slicing back at him. I avoided his eyes and looked only at his body, attempting to predict each of his moves.

Then, very suddenly, it all went wrong.

Hob lunged forward with even greater ferocity, and I struggled to defend myself. Had he been holding back until now, just playing with me? I wondered.

He forced me to retreat, and again Ada didn't move fast enough. She was thrown backwards onto the ground. I stumbled and went down on one knee.

Hob ignored me and went straight for Ada, stabbing with both blades.

I'd always thought I was fast – the fastest and the best. Now I proved that it was true.

Somehow I got between Hob and Ada – though there was a price to be paid for this move.

Hob's blade cut my cheek open from eye to earlobe. The wound was deep and I felt the blood gush out. Now I would have two scars, but this one would be much deeper.

Hob took a couple of steps backwards and gave me a superior smile. 'Now I will take another piece of your flesh!' he gloated.

But I knew what I had to do, even though it carried a terrible risk. Hob was so fast I knew I might not manage it without losing my life.

I dived and rolled forward between Hob's legs, cutting upwards with both blades, committing myself to the Mihalick Manoeuvre – the Death Gambit.

THE WHEEL OF REVENGE

For the female of the species is more deadly than
the male.

The Compendium of Ancient Tales and Ballads

HOB

There was pain and darkness. But then, within that darkness, consciousness began, like the first flicker of candlelight
illuminating a crypt.

The pain increased as awareness grew, and finally a muscle convulsed.

With a supreme effort, Hob opened his eyes.

At first he could see nothing; all was silent. But he could
feel the cold wind upon his face and sense a movement somewhere above him in the darkness. He gathered what energy
he could to create some light.

The horizon was sharply curved, as if he was standing on a
small hill – an artificial mound like those once used by the
ancients to inter their dead. Beyond its rim he could see
points of light.

He seemed to be a little way above this mound, and he

tried – and failed – to make sense of it. He searched his memory, but it was fragmented. However, he did remember an enemy, a formidable enemy. Not merely one. There had been many enemies.

There was memory of defeat; memory of pain; memory of dismemberment.

He realized then that he had neither arms nor legs; not even a torso. He turned his gaze inwards, searching down into his innermost being, searching for the gorestad, the high mind.

Then he knew the ultimate pain – the pain of final defeat. There was no gorestad. He was just one self; he was all that remained. He had been mutilated and scattered so widely that he could no longer be regenerated.

It was then that Hob recognized the dark shapes wheeling far above him . . .

The vulture moved closer to the carrion. It was a scavenger, and would normally have waited for its prey to die. But this prey was helpless and almost immobile. It took three strides forward, spread its wings wide and fixed the sky with a hard stare. It raised its ruff of feathers, signalling dominion – claiming ownership of the meat below.

The other scavengers were already gliding closer in long widdershins spirals. They were not daunted by this display. They would all taste this flesh.

Seeing the intent of its fellows, the vulture flapped its wings and half flew, half hopped onto the head, which was impaled on the sharp broken flagpole. Its claws pierced the bald crown, and the ravening beak came down, seeking the flesh within the left eye-socket.

As it did so, Hob's mouth opened wide in a silent scream. Soon the other scavengers had gathered to squabble over the meat.

When the sun finally rose above the dome of the Wheel, Hob's head had been picked to the bone and the vultures had already flown west to their usual gathering place on the roof of the huge slaughterhouse. There they would live well on offal until sunset.

All day the sun shone upon the head stuck on the flagpole of the Wheel's dome. At first it gleamed white, but gradually it grew darker; by evening flesh once more covered the bone.

Full regeneration was impossible, but the impulse was there. Energy was drawn from the sun itself. Only when the mind of Hob could once again monitor the process would the futility be apparent.

At last the sun dipped below the horizon and night fell.

There was pain and darkness. But then, within that darkness, consciousness began, like the first flicker of candlelight illuminating a crypt.

The pain increased as awareness grew, and finally a muscle convulsed.

With a supreme effort, Hob opened his eyes – and saw the vultures circling above.

The first one flapped its wings and half flew, half hopped onto his head. Helpless, he felt its talons pierce his bald crown. The ravening beak came down, seeking the flesh within his left eye-socket.

Screaming silently, Hob was carried forward once more in agony, tortured upon the wheel of Kwin's revenge.

THE EMISSARY

Those who step into an arena should beware; there
may be greater and more deadly zones of combat
than that of the Trigladius; and there too endoff
may be called.

Amabramdata: the Genthai Book of Prophecy

LEIF

It was already spring: tomorrow night the Arena 13 season
would begin. I'd trained hard and was in peak condition. I
was looking forward to my first contest.

I was having breakfast with Kwin and Ada when the mes-
senger rapped on the front door. He was a young Genthai
warrior, sent by Konnit to bring me to the northern edge
of the city, where he was waiting for me. I had to leave at
once.

Once I would have asked Tyron's permission, but he was
dead and the house seemed emptier than ever. Kwin and
Teena still mourned their father. I mourned Tyron and poor
Deinon, but life went on. Ada was now managing and training Tyron's stable of combatants and their lacs.

'I'm coming with you, Leif!' Kwin said; her expression brooked no argument. 'Last time Konnit sent for you, you ended up staying away for months. This time I want a say in what happens.'

'Then I will come too,' said Ada. 'I'd like to see what's so important that you aren't even allowed to finish your breakfast.'

We headed north. It was just starting to get light, though the sun had not yet risen. As we approached the road that led out of the city, I saw a small crowd of people – amongst them a score of mounted Genthai warriors. A tall figure carrying two longswords at his hips turned and came towards us.

There was no mistaking him. It was Konnit.

'You have a visitor, Leif,' he told me. 'She asked for you by name. She calls herself Peri and has come to us through the Barrier.'

I saw Ada and Kwin looking at me in astonishment. They knew what Peri was – the communicator of a djinni; the self that interacted with others on behalf of the total entity. Ada had told me that all such communicators were called by that name, but as we drew nearer, I saw that it was *my* Peri – the one I'd come to know well on my recent journey beyond the Barrier.

As I approached her, she gazed at me serenely. As always, her black hair was braided with green stones. I looked at her long graceful neck and noted that the gills at her throat had disappeared. This time she had not swum down the River Medie. Behind her I could see the replica of my horse, Laras; another aspect of the djinni Shalatan.

Peri came forward with a warm smile and seized my right

hand in hers. She stroked the back of my hand with her thumb, performing the handshake, but then stepped back and stared at me, her brown eyes full of sadness. 'Why have you not come to join us?' she asked. 'Why have you not led your people to the High Wall?'

Out of the corner of my eye I saw Konnit looking at me. She had addressed me as if I was the leader of the Genthai.

I didn't know how to reply. I waited for Konnit to answer for me, but then, as the silence lengthened, Peri spoke again.

'Many enemy djinn gather north of the wall – among them asscka, with legions of barska and orla. Without your help we cannot hold the gate for long. My lady asks that you come now, before it is too late.'

'This is surely a battle that we cannot hope to win,' Konnit said, his voice full of authority.

'You have no choice,' Peri said, still staring into my eyes. 'The asscka know that you slew the barska and orla. They cannot forgive that. Nor can they forgive humans for leaving Danur, the place assigned to them. Once they breach the wall and defeat my lady, they will come to Gindeen – to kill all humans and destroy your city. Are you not warriors?' she demanded imperiously. 'It is better to fight than wait to die.'

It has taken almost three weeks to gather our army together and reach the Barrier.

At the core of this army are the Genthai, with their elite mounted archers. But the city has its own militia too – over three thousand strong – and there is a force of over two hundred feral lacs led by Thrym.

In spite of our reservations, both Ada and Kwin will come with us. They argued that there was no point in leaving them behind. If we were defeated, the djinn would soon reach Gindeen and raze it to the ground. This time they would kill every human.

I cannot see how we may prevail. I know Konnit feels the same – though he never speaks of defeat because it is not the Genthai way. But with us we take twelve sealed wagons, each containing the weapon feared by all djinn – the gramagandar. The thirteenth weapon, exhausted after exhaling its final breath, remains near the underground lair of Hob's dead shateks.

I wondered how Shalatan would feel if she knew we possessed such weapons and were prepared to use them. Konnit wanted to tell Peri, but Ada advised against it. The use of the gramagandar is anathema to all djinn; an abomination that fills them with loathing.

Peri has gone ahead now, returning to join her other selves. She has no need to tell them of our decision to accede to her request. What she knows is known instantaneously by *all* the selves of Shalatan because of the gorestad, the high mind. They are one entity – a warrior djinni.

Tomorrow, with the help of the Medes, we will begin to cross the Barrier. Not all of us will pass through safely. I fear that Kwin will be taken from me and have insisted that I am next to her when we cross.

Many good people have died: Kern, Tal, Garrett, Tyron, Wode and Deinon. I miss them all. Soon we will ride across the stone bridge where Garrett was slain. He did not live to see this, but he helped to make it possible.

Humans are about to ride forth to do battle with the djinn.

Maybe we *are* what I called out so arrogantly to the barska and orla.

We are the Beast from Danur.

We ride to take back our world.

THE MIDGARD GLOSSARY

This glossary has been compiled from the following primary sources:

> *The Manual of Nym*
> *The Testimony of Math*
> *The Manual of Trigladius Combat*
> *Amabramsum: the Genthai Book of Wisdom*
> *Amabramdata: the Genthai Book of Prophecy*
> *The Compendium of Ancient Tales and Ballads*
> *The History of the Conflict* by Eitel the Pessimist

ADA AUGUSTA

The High Adept of the Imperial Academy, who was slain by djinn terrorists at the beginning of the First Insurrection. Her soul was placed in Containment. She was named after Ada Augusta, Countess of Lovelace, who wrote the very first computer algorithm.

ADJUDICATOR

A type of djinni responsible for overseeing all forms of djinn combat, from those in the arena to battles of open warfare. They rarely show themselves to the participants until the combat is over, when their gungara absorb the blood of the weakest. By that means do they profit from their labours, and their shateks are the most proficient and prolific of all, generating shapes with ease.

Although performing a similar function, the Chief Marshal, he who oversees combat within Arena 13, is not a true Adjudicator. He is just a barbarian human.

AFICIONADOS

These are the devotees of the Trigladius; spectators whose knowledge of the proceedings – of the positions adopted by lacs and their tactical manoeuvres – is often greater than that of some combatants. Some specialize in the history of the Trigladius and can remember classic encounters of long ago by recalling, step by step, the patterns that led to victory.

AGNWAN

The agnwan, known by barbarians as a horse, is a cowardly beast unsuitable for use in warfare. It undoubtedly has a certain grace, but it is outside the wurde and belongs to an age when the fecundity of nature was haphazard and chance spawned strange forms of life, each lone small mind encapsulated within a single host of flesh.

AMABRAMDATA

This is *The Genthai Book of Prophecy*. Although this holy book is written by a multitude of Genthai authors, it is believed that it represents the voice of their god, Thangandar.

AMABRAMSUM

This is the name of *The Genthai Book of Wisdom*. It contains observations on djinn, Midgard and the world before the fall of the ur-humans. This is the collective wisdom of Genthai scribes. It is not a holy book.

ARENA 13

This is another name for the Trigladius Arena. Once it was compulsory for human combatants in this arena to have the number 13 tattooed upon their foreheads. Once this rule was rescinded, it was still fashionable for many years, but the custom is now dying out.

ARTIFICERS

These are adepts skilled in patterning the wurdes of Nym. The first artificers were ur-human, and they developed their power to its height in the Secondary Epoch of Empire. Asscka, the most advanced form of djinni, are now the greatest artificers, having total control of Nym and the ability to shape themselves. The poorest artificers are barbarian humans, who pattern lacs who lack sentience. They build into them the steps of the dance that informs Trigladius combat in Arena 13.

ASGARD

In Norse mythology, this signifies the Place Where the Gods Dwell. Some inhabitants of Midgard use this name to signify the place beyond the Barrier, which is the rest of the Earth occupied by the djinn.

ASSCKA

Asscka are the highest classification of djinn. These are true shape-shifters and, unless limited by the wurde, can number up to 10,000 selves and scores of shateks. During the Tertiary Epoch of Empire, djinn grew in power and ur-human artificer control of them diminished.

BARGE MASTERS

The barge masters are responsible for overseeing the transit of goods from the Sea Gate down the canal to Gindeen. There are seven of them, working a shift rota.

BARRIER

The Great Barrier is the zone of mist, darkness and fear that encircles Midgard, preventing entry or exit. Those who approach too closely either never come back or return insane. The Trader passes through the Barrier unharmed, but he makes the journey by sea.

BARSK

A barsk is the higher partner of a binary warrior djinni. Four-armed, with keen sight and great ferocity, his mount, and partner, is the orl, a two-legged creature with hands capable of wielding weapons. Barsk and orl were created each for the other; the first has a higher mind and greater access to the gorestad, which they share unequally. The barsk is dominant yet still dependent upon that which carries it. Such binary djinn are born of a shatek but lack the power to be born again. By this limitation were they shaped as warriors, for those who can die only once fight most fiercely to hold onto life.

BINARY DJINN

Binary djinn are the next rank above singletons. Theirs is a symbiotic relationship, but this partnership of two is not always equal as in the case of bàrsk and orl.

CATARA

Catara are sea-djinn which take two basic forms. The first are crustacea, with hard shells and many legs, which live close to the shore; the second are cephalopods with eight arms and two tentacles, which inhabit deep water. Both were developed by ur-humans for purposes of warfare.

CHACCKAN

This is the djinn title for *Lord*, which is used to address those who hold high rank north of the wall.

CHIEF MARSHAL

This official is the highest authority within the Wheel, with many assistant marshals to enforce his decisions. The main focus of his attention is Arena 13 where he supervises combat. Although his function in that arena may seem largely ceremonial, in the case of any dispute his decision is absolute and there can be no appeal.

COMMONALITY

This is the name given to the underground zone beneath the Wheel where lacs are stored by owners who cannot afford to lease private quarters.

COMPENDIUM OF ANCIENT TALES AND BALLADS, THE

This is a compilation of writings by humans before the fall and the subsequent construction of the Barrier. They take the form of lyrics, poems and prose fragments. Most are without a named author.

CONTAINMENT

This is the digital store within which a soul is preserved with the possibility of being born again into a body of false flesh. An alternative name for this condition is 'Stasis'.

COVENANT

The Covenant is the agreement made between the djinn and mankind following the defeat of the latter. Humans were set down within the confines of the Barrier and given a chance to live there, providing that they accepted the rule of the Protector. The Genthai were to submit to ritual culling by the werewights; Non-Genthai were to accept culling by Hob. As time passed the Covenant was forgotten about by city dwellers. Some believe that no such agreement was ever made.

CYRO

He was the official responsible for the Commonality, the large underground zone below the Wheel. With the help of a small army of assistants, he supervised the storage of lacs, the kitchens, the training areas and the combat zones. Cyro ruled his domain with absolute authority and nobody interfered in his activities, some of which were illegal. Cyro was slain by Thrym.

DANUR

This is the djinn name for Midgard. It means the Place of the Beast. A legend tells of a beast of great ferocity that is imprisoned there behind the cloud which humans call the Barrier. Another name for it is *Kisetorian Dutred*.

DECIDONS

Decidons are hybrid djinn with ten selves, containing elements of both animal and vegetable but resembling trees. Largely static, they communicate by wind-blown pollen. Ur-humans developed them as sentinels and also for purposes of espionage. They have offensive capabilities and generate both poisons and antidotes.

DJINNi

A djinni is the wurde made flesh. The different types of djinn are more numerous than the visible stars. They range from low singletons, who may hardly be higher than base simulacra, to high djinn known as asscka, who may now generate selves almost beyond counting. Almost all djinn are subordinate in some way − some major, some minor − to the patterns of the ur-humans who first gave their progenitors shape. But of all these, most deadly is the djinni who is no longer subservient in any way to the wurdes that shaped him. Originally they were created by the military to serve the Human Empire. Djinn is an acronym which stands for *digital janus interface nano node.*

ENDOFF

This is the close-down function called when a blade is inserted into the throat-slit of a lac, which becomes temporarily inoperative. For the min combatant, it signals the end of the contest. All that remains is the ritual cut to the arm of the defeated human combatant.

EXTENSIBILITY

This is a characteristic of Nym which allows a patterner to add new wurdes and features or modify existing ones. The language can be increased by those who have the skill to do so.

FALSE FLESH

False flesh is the derogatory term first used by ur-humans to describe the flesh hosts of any djinn born of the shatek and the wurde. When the war between djinn and ur-humans intensified, the former adopted the term in defiance and proved, victory by victory, its superiority in every way to ur-human flesh.

FIRST INSURRECTION

The First Insurrection began with two terrorist attacks upon humans by the djinn. The first was an attempt upon the life of the Empress, which failed. The second was an attack upon the Imperial Academy, in which over a hundred lives were lost, including that of the High Adept. The djinn rebellion was eventually put down by the employment of the gramagandar, the weapon which dissolves false flesh.

GAMBLING HOUSE

The gambling agents (sometimes known as 'touts') accept wagers on behalf of the large gambling houses which under-pin the economy of Midgard. From their profits fees are paid to combatants who fight from the mag position. Only min combatants are allowed to bet upon themselves – but only to win.

Bets offered to Arena 13 gallery spectators are often very complex. Many aficionados attempt to predict the actual time of a victory and use accumulators, where winnings are placed upon the outcome of succeeding contests. Red tickets are sold, and these bets are made on the likelihood of a con-testant suffering injury or death.

GHETTA

This is a love token traditionally offered to a woman by a Genthai warrior when he asks her to be his wife. If the woman accepts, she shows it to her family. Her father then keeps it as evidence of the man's commitment.

GINDEEN

This is the only city of Midgard, although there are some small towns and hamlets. Gindeen consists largely of wooden buildings, with roads that are just mud tracks. Its main landmarks are the Wheel, the large cube-shaped slaughter-house, and the citadel of Hob, which casts its shadow over the city.

GORESTAD

Gorestad is the 'high mind' usually operative in all high djinn with more than one self. But despite this group consciousness, which makes a djinni with many selves just one entity, there is always some individual awareness particular to each self. Both asscka and shalatan can control the awareness of their selves, even denying particular selves access to gorestad.

GRAMAGANDAR

An ancient weapon, also known as the Breath of the Wolf, the fire of which is capable of dissolving all false flesh. This weapon is anathema to all djinn and its use is forbidden. It was created and deployed by the last ur-humans, and for this crime they were destroyed, their fallen and debased descend- ants, the barbarian humans, banished for all time to Midgard, the place within the Barrier.

GUNGARA

Gungara form the third component of all high djinn. These gungara are winged and are used to devour and absorb the mind and tissue of enemies or other creatures in need of study and/or reanimation by means of the wurde and the shatek. Gungara were not created by ur-humans and are a prime example of djinn self-directed evolution.

HANDSHAKE

When djinn confront each other, a handshake is the name for the preliminary routine exchange of information between them to establish identities and purpose. It is the first stage in protocol to determine either coexistence or conflict. Without a handshake full lethal force is immediately applied.

HANSHA
This means the 'strangers' house'. It is a dwelling built to accommodate visiting representatives of other djinn.

HOB
It is believed that Hob is a rogue djinni who remained within the Barrier when barbarian humans were sealed within it. He preys upon humans, taking their blood and sometimes their minds. He occasionally fights within Arena 13 from the mag position.

HUMANS
Humans are the ur-race of creatures that created the language called Nym, thus constructing the first djinn and preparing the way for those which would supersede them. Outside the wurde, they are termed ur-humans, whereas their fallen and debased descendants are called barbarian humans. These latter are closest in form to the type of singletons known as lacs, though without their strength, speed and coordination. Their strength comes from their ability to cooperate and combine forces for a common purpose. It may also spring from the fear of death, having only one self which can easily be snuffed out in battle.

INDEX
The catalogue of lacs, souls bound within false flesh, and wurdes offered by the Trader on his twice-yearly visits to

Midgard. The Index exists only within the mind of the Trader and there is no written record of its contents.

KRANSIN
This is a substance used to coat the blades of lacs for contests in Arena 13. It is a combined coagulant and an intensifier of pain. Thus the ritual cut suffered by the loser is agonizing. That pain must be faced with courage, as the spectators watching from the gallery judge how the losing combatant conducts himself.

KRIE-KORE
This is a way station or fortress used by warrior djinn when beyond the walls of their cities. Most of it is underground.

LAC
This is an abbreviated form of **simulacrum**. Lacs are born of a shatek for the purposes of arena combat of various types. Although shaped to resemble barbarian humans, they have a throat-slit which, once penetrated by a blade, brings instant unconsciousness, the state called by the wurde endoff. They also have long arms to aid fighting in Arena 13.

LUDUSA
A type of binary djinn who share a gorestad equally. Sometimes having no apparent connection in either appearance or role, they were created by ur-humans for the purpose of espionage.

LUPINA

A category of djinn which take on a variety of wolf shapes. Werewights are a debased and fallen form of this djinn category; they are instinctual rather than rational. However, true lupina are the most intelligent of all djinn.

MANUAL OF NYM, THE

A detailed guide to the patterning language known as Nym and of the wurdes contained in its two dictionaries (known as *Fat Nym* and *Slim Nym*). The latter is a basic reduced version of the former, which is continually extending.

MAORI

These are the ancestor gods of the Genthai, who are believed to live in the sky on a long white cloud.

MEDES

Genthai mystics, known as *Medes*, frequent the vicinity of the Barrier and are sensitive to its fluctuations. They take their name from the River Medie; its banks are the easiest point of entry and exit. Medes have the ability to pass through the barrier unharmed and guide others. The journey is dangerous and not all those escorted survive.

MEDIE

The Medie is a small river that flows out of the Genthai lands and meets the sea not far north of the Sea Gate.

MIDGARD

From Norse mythology, it means the Place Where Men Dwell or the Battlefield of Men. It is the zone allocated to the barbarian humans, the survivors of the fallen empire.

MIHALICK MANOEUVRE

This is commonly known as the *Death Gambit* and consists of a forward roll through the line of opposing lacs (or lac) to cut one's opponent and claim victory. Only Mihalick has successfully completed this risky manoeuvre. Subsequent attempts have resulted in death or maiming.

MUSEUM OF LIGHTS

This museum is reputed to hold a record of images and items from the human civilization that preceded the Fall. Its location is unknown but some believe it is to be found within the Protector's palace.

NEWT

An analytical wurde-tool used by an artificer to explore a wurde-matrix and, if necessary, penetrate defences set up by the original creator of that system. It is far more sophisticated than either **poke** or **peek**.

NYM

Nym evolved from a primitive patterning language called FORTH. It is the language that enabled the creation of the first djinn. All djinn are the wurde made flesh.

OBUTAYER

The Obutayer is the matriarch who rules the Genthai in times of peace. When the tribe are on a war-footing their leader is a male warrior.

OMPHALOS

This is the centre post of the Wheel. Cut from a tree of great height and girth, it is considered by some to be the very centre of Midgard and the hub of the Wolf Wheel.

OTHER

The 'Other' is the term used by a djinni for those not numbered amongst its own selves. Only by protocol can djinn achieve cooperation. Only by combat can they know their position.

PEEK

A basic Nym wurde-tool which is used to read elements of patterns and how they are linked.

POKE

A basic Nym wurde-tool which is used to insert other wurdes or primitives into a pattern.

PRIMITIVES

Primitives are the building blocks from which a wurde is constructed.

PROTECTOR, THE

The ruler of Midgard. He was placed there by the djinn from beyond the Barrier and is answerable to them. His role is to keep order, and for this he has an armed guard of several thousand men who mainly confine themselves to the city of Gindeen and the surrounding area.

Some believe that the Protector is the same one who was appointed when the Human Empire fell and the remnants were placed within the Barrier. Others believe that he is a djinni.

PROTOCOL

Protocol is the name for the communication rituals, both physical and of the wurde, by means of which djinn coexist without constant bloodletting. Protocol, once completed successfully, is known as a handshake.

QUEUE

This is a long sequence of wurdes held within the mind of a lac. Called by a single wurde, this can result in highly complex behaviour which has been determined in advance by the patterner.

RASIRE

A type of low-level singleton, approximately human in shape, used by other djinn as beasts of burden. Having offensive capabilities, they are also used in battle, but mostly held in reserve. They are difficult to control and are inclined to rebel against authority.

RECARDA

Recarda are warrior djinn developed by ur-humans for combat in cold climes. They have six legs and can run on ice or snow at great speed. Their triple-hinged jaws are capable of extreme leverage so that no armour is proof against them.

RESPITE HOUSE

A refuge for widows who have lost their husbands in Arena 13, it is a charitable organization mostly funded by the wealthier artificers. Not usually a permanent residence, it does provide overnight accommodation where women can offer emotional comfort to each other and ease the pain of bereavement.

ROMANA

This is the name given to the Second Epoch of the Human Empire. Gladiatorial combat between djinn became the chief form of mass entertainment, and it became fashionable to associate it with the forms, names and behaviour of an ancient primitive human nation called Rome which spoke a language known as Latin. Thus many high-born families adopted Roman names. The terms Trigladius and Gladius are typical Latinate constructs.

SECOND INSURRECTION

The Second Insurrection was a coordinated surprise attack upon humans by all djinn. Human civilization fell, but a few thousand survivors were allowed to live and breed within a specially designated area surrounded by a Barrier. This reserve was designated Midgard.

SELF

A sentient component of a djinni; it is a host of false flesh born of a shatek.

SHALATAN

A second-rank djinni just below an asscka. The number of a shalatan is 713 and it has only one large shatek. Consequently, it takes time to regenerate selves slain in battle. This military djinni, created to wage war, is always ruled by a self which takes the human female form. If favoured, such a ruler becomes the concubine of an asscka. A shalatan has great skill in generating selves to perform particular tasks. One such self is known as a peri, which functions as ambassador to other djinn. A peri is skilled in understanding the 'Other' and is proficient in languages.

SHAPE-SHIFTERS

This is a category to which all high djinn belong. To change the form of a self takes time, ranging from hours to weeks depending upon the degree of change required. Preceding this process, high intakes of food are necessary, the most useful being blood taken directly from living creatures. The more usual method of shape-shifting is through use of the wurde and the shatek to generate selves for particular tasks.

SHATEK

A shatek is the mother of a djinni. The midwife is a Nym artificer who shapes the offspring using wurdes of Nym.

SINGLETON

A singleton is a djinni with only one self. This is the lowest form, a being superior to the barbarian human only in speed, strength and reflexes. Yet some singletons have great intellectual capacity and can, by disciplined study of the wurde, elevate themselves to higher forms. A sub-form of singleton is known as a **lac**.

STACK

The stack is a defensive tri-glad tactic in which the human combatant is sandwiched between two defending lacs which rotate like a wheel according to the dictates of combat.

The stack is also the term for a sequence of Nym code to which a patterner might add or subtract. New code is always placed at the summit of a stack.

SYCODA

These are djinn with multiple selves but a limited capacity to generate more. They are shape-shifters and have skills which make them good interrogators. Spying and torture are their main functions. Hob belongs to this category but has cast off many of the constraints that once limited his development.

TASSELS

This is the name given to those who dwell on the fringes of Hob's citadel and sometimes within it, serving his needs. Some are related to Hob's victims and serve him hoping for news of their loved ones; some belong to a cult which worships Hob, hoping that one day he will return their wives, daughters or sons to them in perfect new bodies. Others are spies who scratch out a living by supplying Hob with information or acting as go-betweens in contacts with certain citizens of Gindeen.

It is the behaviour of this last group which resulted in the name tassels, which are fringed knots on the hem of Hob's cloak. The name was given in mockery because they are a fallen and degraded group, but the idea of knots is appropriate because they are also part of the tangle of conspiracy and counter-conspiracy as the various groups within Midgard struggle to achieve their goals.

TESTIMONY OF MATH, THE
A book written by Math, the hero of Arena 13. It documents his early training and deals at length with each of his contests against the djinni Hob.

TRADER
The Trader is Midgard's only source of lacs and new wurdes of Nym to enhance the patterning of lacs. He usually visits the Sea Gate twice a year: before the season begins and then halfway through it.

TRIGLADIUS
This is fought within Arena 13, the highest level of combat within the Wheel. Three lacs face a lone lac in a contest where victory results from the spilling of human blood. A human combatant stands behind the three in what is known as the 'mag' position; his opponent stands behind the lone lac in the 'min' position. They present themselves as targets for

their opponent's lacs. Victory is marked by a ritual cut to the arm of the defeated combatant. Although the intention is not to kill, accidents do happen. In addition, grudge matches are fought which end in the decapitation of the loser.

ULUM

This is a sound-code used within the Trigladius Arena to communicate with and direct a lac, delivered by taps of the combatant's boots on the arena floor. Each combatant develops his own version of Ulum and keeps it a secret.

WEREWIGHT

This is a creature with four selves but a high mind. Three take the form of wolves, but the fourth stands upright and is a mixture of human and wolf. The Genthai fight this creature in ritual combat every thirteen years. Some believe it to be a type of fallen, degraded djinni. Others think this might well have been the origin of Trigladius combat in Arena 13.

WHEEL

The Wheel is situated in the barbarian human city of Gindeen, within the Barrier. It is a building where gladiatorial contests take place between lacs. It has thirteen combat zones, and the highest and most skilful of these is the Trigladius, which is also known as Arena 13.

WHEEL DIRECTORATE

The Wheel Directorate had a membership of five, composed of representatives of the gambling houses and headed by Pyncheon, the Chief Marshal. Its primary jurisdiction was over the Wheel, but it had wider legal powers. In the city of Gindeen it was second only to the Protector, but concentrated mostly on the business of the Wheel. For example, a killing in the streets in which a combatant or ex-combatant was involved would fall under its remit.

After the fall of the Protector, the Wheel Directorate was renamed the City Directorate. Then, following an alliance with the Genthai, it became the Ruling Council, which governed the whole of Midgard.

WURDE

The wurde is the basic unit within the ancient patterning language called Nym. Wurdes contain other wurdes, and to call one wurde is to call all that are embedded.

JOSEPH DELANEY

 facebook.com/**josephdelaneybooks**

josephdelaneyauthor

Read on for a sneak peek of the latest instalment
in Joseph Delaney's bestselling Spook's series,
Dark Assassin

CHAPTER 1
SPOOK'S BUSINESS

THOMAS WARD

I accompanied Alice to the edge of the garden, where we halted and kissed goodbye.

'Take care,' I begged her. 'I don't know what I'd do without you.'

Alice was just about the prettiest girl I'd ever seen, but now there was sadness in her beautiful eyes. She felt the same way as I did: we didn't want to be apart.

She was off to Pendle once more to try to form an alliance with the witches there. She'd already made two failed attempts. The three main clans – the Malkins, the Deanes and the Mouldheels – didn't get on. Well, that was to seriously understate the situation. There was rivalry and hatred between them; sometimes they even fought and killed each other. But an alliance between these clans and us was vital if we were to defend the County against the magic of the Kobalos mages.

The witch clans had formed alliances before, so I knew it was possible, and Alice was optimistic. I had to hope.

The dark army of the bestial Kobalos was approaching the far shore of the Northern Sea, their malicious gaze fixed upon our own country. But there was an even more immediate danger. Using powerful magic, their High Mages were able to project themselves directly into the County. They could bring a few warriors with them and attack at any time.

By now the military were aware of the army and the County was on a war footing against the threat of invasion. Forces from the two main barracks, at Burnley and Colne, had marched east to fortify the border. Those that remained were stretched thin, fighting off Kobalos raids. People were scared, and travel was dangerous.

The Kobalos mages had also tried to summon Golgoth, the Lord of Winter, into the County. Had they succeeded, we would have been plunged into a permanent winter, the countryside left frozen and weakened by famine. Only with the help of the Old God, Pan, and Alice's powerful magic had we managed to prevent that. Despite this, I'd never felt so vulnerable; never felt less able to do my duty and protect the County from the dark.

'You take care too, Tom. Ain't going to be away for more than a week, I promise you,' Alice told me now.

We hugged, kissed again, and then she set off for Pendle. She was wearing a green dress and a short brown jacket as protection against the chill air. It was early spring, but as yet there was little warmth in the sun. As she walked away, I glanced down at her pointy shoes, the mark of a witch. Alice had finally gone to the dark, but she wasn't a witch who practised bone, blood or familiar magic – she was an earth witch, perhaps the first one ever. She served Pan and drew her magic from the Earth itself.

Just before she reached the edge of the slope, she turned and waved to me. I waved back, and then she was out of sight. Already missing her, I turned back to the garden and headed for the practice post.

As I did so, I saw a silver chain falling towards it, spinning widdershins – against the clock. It formed a spiral, tightening upon the post in the classic manner, achieving a perfect spread from top to bottom. Had that post been a witch, she would have been bound from head to knee, the chain tightening hard against her teeth to prevent her from chanting spells.

'Well done, Jenny!' I called out.

Jenny was my apprentice. I knew that my own master, John Gregory, would never have taken her on. To become a spook's apprentice you had to be a seventh son of a seventh son.

Jenny was a girl; as far as I knew, she was the first girl ever to have been trained by a spook. She claimed to be a seventh daughter of a seventh daughter, but I'd never been able to verify that because she'd been brought up by foster parents. Still, I could not deny that she had gifts that were useful when fighting the dark – different ones from mine. She could make herself almost invisible and possessed such great empathy that she could almost read people's minds.

I looked at her as she stood there smiling. Her face was freckled and she had different-coloured eyes – the left was blue, the right one green.

'Well, what's your score?' I demanded.

'I've managed fifteen successes in twenty attempts! A

couple more weeks of this and I'll be better than you!' she said cheekily.

That success rate was good, but I would have preferred a little more respect from my apprentice. The trouble was, I was only two years older than her; in August I'd be eighteen and she'd be sixteen. We even shared the same birthday – the third. My own apprenticeship had come to a premature end when my master had been killed fighting enemy witches.

Suddenly a sound drew our attention. It was the pealing of the bell at the withy trees crossroads. Our garden was guarded by the boggart, Kratch, which meant that it was dangerous for outsiders to venture in, so those in need of help stayed clear; they usually went to the crossroads and summoned me by ringing the bell.

'It's spook's business,' I said softly.

The last couple of days had been quiet, but I'd known that it couldn't last. There were always local threats from the dark in the County. This time the danger might come from the Kobalos.

'Can I come with you?' Jenny asked.

'No, Jenny, it's best that I go alone. You carry on practising here. You'll need to work a lot harder if you want to be as good as me!'

Here in the garden the boggart would keep her safe against most things, I knew. Beyond its boundaries it was a different matter.

I was carrying my staff, but I also had the powerful Starblade in a scabbard on my back. As long as I held it or had it on my person, dark magic couldn't harm me.

'But if it means a journey, can I go with you to sort out the problem?' Jenny persisted.

My apprentice had to be trained, and that meant sharing the danger of our craft. So I nodded and, with a grin, she went to retrieve my silver chain and prepared to cast it at the post again. I supposed that I had to let her learn, just as I had . . .

As I strode out of the garden and headed towards the sound of that pealing bell, a wave of sadness washed over me. Things had changed so much since I'd begun my own apprenticeship. Not only was my master, John Gregory, dead; Grimalkin, the assassin of the Malkin clan, had been slain by Golgoth. Although she was a witch, she'd been a strong and powerful ally who had taken the lead in fighting the Kobalos. I would almost go so far as to say that she had become a friend. She'd certainly saved my life on several occasions. It was Grimalkin who had forged the Starblade for me, and then trained me in its use. She would be greatly missed.

As I walked, I glanced up at the fells that rose far above the village – Parlick Pike and Wolf Fell. Their summits were still white with snow which sparkled in the sunlight.

As I reached the withy trees, the pealing of the bell ceased. Whoever was ringing it must have heard my approach. People were often nervous when waiting to speak to a spook, not sure what to expect from the man who wore a cloak and carried a staff and a silver chain. Sometimes those nerves got the better of them and they left before I arrived.

I headed into the shade of the trees and saw a stocky figure standing by the bellrope, which was dancing and swaying at his side. He wore a black gown and hood and even carried a staff – he was dressed like a spook! Who could it be? This man was surely too broad to be Judd Brinscall, who worked the territory north of Caster.

I halted close to him, and he suddenly pulled back his hood to reveal his face.

The shock of what I saw took my breath away.

It was impossible.

I was gazing at a dead man . . .